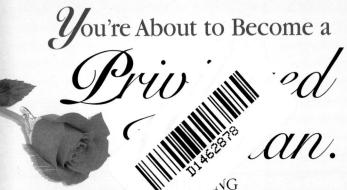

You're About to Become a
Privileged Woman.

INTRODUCING

PAGES & PRIVILEGES™.

It's our way of thanking you for buying
our books at your favorite retail store.

GET ALL THIS FREE
WITH JUST ONE PROOF OF PURCHASE:

◆ **Hotel Discounts up to 60% at home and abroad**

◆ **Travel Service - Guaranteed lowest published
   airfares plus 5% cash back on tickets**

◆ **$25 Travel Voucher**

◆ **Sensuous Petite Parfumerie collection ($50 value)**

◆ **Insider Tips Letter with sneak previews of
   upcoming books**

◆ **Mystery Gift (if you enroll before 6/15/95)**

*You'll get a FREE personal card, too.
It's your passport to all these benefits– and to
even more great gifts & benefits to come!*

There's no club to join. No purchase commitment. No obligation.

As a *Privileged Woman,* you'll be entitled to all these *Free Benefits.* And *Free Gifts,* too.

To thank you for buying our books, we've designed an exclusive FREE program called *PAGES & PRIVILEGES™*. You can enroll with just one Proof of Purchase, and get the kind of luxuries that, until now, you could only read about.

*B*IG HOTEL DISCOUNTS

A privileged woman stays in the finest hotels. And so can you—at up to 60% off! Imagine standing in a hotel check-in line and watching as the guest in front of you pays $150 for the same room that's only costing you $60. Your *Pages & Privileges* discounts are good at Sheraton, Marriott, Best Western, Hyatt and thousands of other fine hotels all over the U.S., Canada and Europe.

*F*REE DISCOUNT TRAVEL SERVICE

A privileged woman is always jetting to romantic places. When <u>you</u> fly, just make one phone call for the lowest published airfare at time of booking—<u>or double the difference back</u>! PLUS—

you'll get a $25 voucher to use the first time you book a flight AND <u>5% cash back on every ticket you buy thereafter through the travel service</u>!

𝓕REE GIFTS!

A privileged woman is always getting wonderful gifts.
Luxuriate in rich fragrances that will stir your senses (and his). This gift-boxed assortment of fine perfumes includes three popular scents, each in a beautiful designer bottle.   <u>Truly Lace</u>...This luxurious fragrance unveils your sensuous side. <u>L'Effleur</u>...discover the romance of the Victorian era with this soft floral. <u>Muguet des bois</u>...a single note floral of singular beauty. This $50 value is yours—FREE when you enroll in *Pages & Privileges* ! And it's just the beginning of the gifts and benefits that will be coming your way!

𝓕REE INSIDER TIPS LETTER

A privileged woman is always informed. And you'll be, too, with our free letter full of fascinating information and sneak previews of upcoming books.

𝓜ORE GREAT GIFTS & BENEFITS TO COME

A privileged woman always has a lot to look forward to.
And so will you. You get all these wonderful FREE gifts and benefits now with only one purchase...and there are no additional purchases required. However, each additional retail purchase of Harlequin and Silhouette books brings you a step closer to even more great FREE benefits like half-price movie tickets...and even more FREE gifts like these beautiful fragrance gift baskets:

L'Effleur ...This basketful of romance lets you discover L'Effleur from head to toe, heart to home.

Truly Lace ...A basket spun with the sensuous luxuries of Truly Lace, including Dusting Powder in a reusable satin and lace covered box.

𝓔NROLL 𝓝OW!
Complete the Enrollment Form on the back of this card and become a Privileged Woman today!

Enroll Today in *PAGES & PRIVILEGES*™, the program that gives you Great Gifts and Benefits with just one purchase!

Enrollment Form

☐ *Yes!* I WANT TO BE A *P*RIVILEGED *W*OMAN.

Enclosed is one *PAGES & PRIVILEGES*™ Proof of Purchase from any Harlequin or Silhouette book currently for sale in stores (Proofs of Purchase are found on the back pages of books) and the store cash register receipt. Please enroll me in *PAGES & PRIVILEGES*™. Send my Welcome Kit and FREE Gifts -- and activate my FREE benefits -- immediately.

NAME (please print)

ADDRESS   APT. NO

CITY   STATE   ZIP/POSTAL CODE

PROOF OF PURCHASE

Please allow 6-8 weeks for delivery. Quantities are limited. We reserve the right to substitute items. Enroll before October 31, 1995 and receive one full year of benefits.

NO CLUB!
NO COMMITMENT!
Just one purchase brings you great **Free Gifts** *and* **Benefits!**
(See inside for details.)

Name of store where this book was purchased_____

Date of purchase_____

Type of store:

☐ Bookstore   ☐ Supermarket   ☐ Drugstore

☐ Dept. or discount store (e.g. K-Mart or Walmart)

☐ Other (specify)_____

Which Harlequin or Silhouette series do you usually read?

_____

Complete and mail with one Proof of Purchase and store receipt to:

U.S.: *PAGES & PRIVILEGES*™, P.O. Box 1960, Danbury, CT 06813-1960

Canada: *PAGES & PRIVILEGES*™, 49-6A The Donway West, P.O. 813, North York, ON M3C 2E8   PRINTED IN U.S.A

***Kell's eyes were lit with warmth
and enchantment, all because
of a baby's smile....***

Jamey's baby's smile.

Oh, my heavens was all Jamey could think. A stirring started way down inside, an involuntary reaction to this man. If there was something in men's genes that made them pursue the female sex, then there was an equally powerful force in women. It was part of the mating dance, Jamey realized, that circling of one another, assessing, evaluating. Courting.

Suddenly she wanted to tell Kell that the baby was hers, that she'd borne a child and could bear more. She wanted to list, bluntly and brazenly, all the qualities that would make her a desirable mate. *A good wife,* she thought, surprising herself.

Dear Reader,

Spring is the perfect time to celebrate the joy of new romance. So get set to fall in love as Silhouette Romance brings you six new wonderful books.

Blaine O'Connor is a *Father in the Making* in Marie Ferrarella's heartwarming FABULOUS FATHERS title. When this handsome bachelor suddenly becomes a full-time dad, he's more than happy to take a few lessons in child rearing from pretty Bridgette Rafanelli. Now he hopes to teach Bridgette a thing or two about love!

Love—Western style—begins this month with a delightful new series, WRANGLERS AND LACE. Each book features irresistible cowboys and the women who tame their wild hearts. The fun begins with *Daddy Was a Cowboy* by Jodi O'Donnell.

In Carolyn Zane's humorous duet, SISTER SWITCH, twin sisters change places and find romance. This time around, sister number two, Emily Brant, meets her match when she pretends sexy Tyler Newroth is her husband in *Weekend Wife*.

Also this month, look for *This Man and This Woman,* an emotional story by Lucy Gordon about a wedding planner who thinks marriage is strictly business—until she meets a dashing Prince Charming of her own. And don't miss *Finally a Family*, Moyra Tarling's tale of a man determined to win back his former love—and be a father to the child he never knew he had. And Margaret Martin makes her debut with *Husband in Waiting*.

Happy Reading!

Anne Canadeo
Senior Editor

Please address questions and book requests to:
Silhouette Reader Service
U.S.: 3010 Walden Ave., P.O. Box 1325, Buffalo, NY 14269
Canadian: P.O. Box 609, Fort Erie, Ont. L2A 5X3

DADDY WAS A COWBOY

Jodi O'Donnell

Silhouette
R O M A N C E™
Published by Silhouette Books
America's Publisher of Contemporary Romance

If you purchased this book without a cover you should be aware that this book is stolen property. It was reported as "unsold and destroyed" to the publisher, and neither the author nor the publisher has received any payment for this "stripped book."

For working mothers everywhere—although if you are a mother, you're working!

Acknowledgments:
Many thanks to the West Texas women who graciously educated this Midwestern sodbuster about ranching: Marva Jean Chisum, Colleen Wheeler, Melanie McGouran and especially Jackye Plummer.

 SILHOUETTE BOOKS

ISBN 0-373-19080-8

DADDY WAS A COWBOY

Copyright © 1995 by Data Analysis and Results Inc.

All rights reserved. Except for use in any review, the reproduction or utilization of this work in whole or in part in any form by any electronic, mechanical or other means, now known or hereafter invented, including xerography, photocopying and recording, or in any information storage or retrieval system, is forbidden without the written permission of the editorial office, Silhouette Books, 300 East 42nd Street, New York, NY 10017 U.S.A.

All characters in this book have no existence outside the imagination of the author and have no relation whatsoever to anyone bearing the same name or names. They are not even distantly inspired by any individual known or unknown to the author, and all incidents are pure invention.

This edition published by arrangement with Harlequin Enterprises B.V.

® and TM are trademarks of Harlequin Enterprises B.V., used under license. Trademarks indicated with ® are registered in the United States Patent and Trademark Office, the Canadian Trade Marks Office and in other countries.

Printed in U.S.A.

Books by Jodi O'Donnell

Silhouette Romance

Still Sweet on Him #969
The Farmer Takes a Wife #992
A Man to Remember #1021
Daddy Was a Cowboy #1080

JODI O'DONNELL

grew up one of fourteen children in small-town Iowa. As a result, she loves to explore in her writing how family relationships influence who and why we love as we do. She is married to the hometown boy she's known since fifth grade. Consequently, Jodi and her husband, Darrel, have no secrets from each other. Together they run a successful consulting business near Dallas, Texas, with the aid of their wolf-hybrid dog, Rio.

Dear Reader,

Cowboy. The word calls up quite an image, doesn't it?

A black Stetson pulled low over inscrutable eyes. A sturdy shoulder with a saddle slung over it. Long, lean legs in well-worn jeans. And don't forget those boots that look like they've walked a hundred miles or more.

But these are just the trappings of a cowboy. In researching *Daddy Was a Cowboy* I went to cattle auctions and feed stores, roundups and rodeos, talked to the men—and women—who ranched in the most hostile conditions Texas can provide: the Panhandle. And I discovered that what makes a real cowboy is his honor and commitment to doing right by the land, animals
and people entrusted to his care. He's a man whose heart is as tender as his hide is tough.

This is the kind of character I wanted to portray. In fact, I wanted to tell the story of both a hero and heroine who discover within themselves—and in each other— the soul of a true cowboy, regardless of gender or experience.

Because these are the men and women who won the West and stole our hearts.

So come on…let's fall in love with a cowboy. Let's be someone a cowboy could fall for.

Jodi O'Donnell

Chapter One

Keller Hamilton set his coffee cup on the counter and squinted at the strange sight outside the kitchen window. Across the windswept ranch yard came...a person. That was the strange part. He didn't know if a man or a woman strode with long legs toward the house. He...she...it was as tall as a man, though a bit on the thin side. As the figure came closer, Kell saw the person was certainly dressed like a man, a cowboy, actually, in well-worn Wrangler jeans and boots scuffed to a dull brown. A swatch of plaid shirt, topped by a blue neckerchief, peeked out from the half-buttoned, sheepskin-lined denim jacket.

Then there was the hat. A shapeless thing with a flattened brim, it looked like it'd been rained on, sat on, stomped on and generally used and abused. It was also crammed down over its occupant's ears and forehead, and largely the reason Kell almost settled on the side of the masculine persuasion.

Yet the ever so slight sway of hips, the set of curved lips beneath the rim of that godawful hat made him suspect, even with evidence to the contrary, that he was looking at a woman. He had to admit he was intrigued.

Kell picked up his coffee and went to greet his guest.

He opened the back door as the person clumped up the outside steps to the enclosed porch, and Kell motioned for him, her, or whomever, to enter the mudroom. The person's chin dropped as Kell guessed that boot soles were being scraped across the hemp rug on the outside step, a gesture of courtesy or habit rather than necessity, since there wasn't an iota of mud on the frozen ground outside. Then the chin came up, and Kell got a clear view through the window in the storm door of a shapely nose, cheeks and chin, and the fineness of skin without a hint of five o'clock shadow. Definitely female, though that was about all he could discern with her hat hiding her face and shadowing her eyes. When she stepped into the porch, he noted just how tall she was. Darned near on a level with his six-foot-three, her nose parallel to his chin. Her full, wide mouth neither frowned nor smiled.

She's nervous, he guessed. And wary. About what?

"Can I help you?" Kell asked, sounding like the Dallas investment broker he'd so recently been. Even with his Lone Star drawl and the Westernisms that were part of every Texan's vocabulary, it'd be a while before he lost the inflection that branded him city-raised.

"I'm lookin' for the owner of this ranch," she said with her own distinct twang. Her voice was rough in pitch, and husky, with a Debra Winger hoarseness a man either found grating or sexy as all get-out. Kell guessed he fit into the latter bunch, and felt a little disconcerted. He'd expected the isolation would have its effects on his libido, but he'd only been here ten days. Not exactly long enough to cause automatic attraction to a woman in the latest from Jed Clampett head wear.

"I'm the owner of Plum Creek Ranch," he said, the words feeling strange on his lips—as if he were telling a white lie. But it was God's truth: he was a rancher now. "Kell Hamilton." And because it seemed natural with this woman in cowboy clothing, he stuck out his hand. She stepped forward and took it, her work glove warm against his palm. His confusion grew as he realized he liked the feel of her hand in his.

"Jamey Dunn, sir. Pleased to meet you." Then she proceeded to churn the life out of his arm like an oil pump-jack run wild. She had a grip like a man's, he'd give her that. A man with something to prove.

After retrieving his thoroughly agitated arm, he asked, "Is there something I can do for you, uh, Jamey?" She didn't look like a Miss Dunn or a Miss Jamey, much less a ma'am, which was the normal form of feminine address around here.

She hesitated. He got the feeling she was sizing him up and down as he'd done her. After a second she said, "Yes, in fact, there is, sir. I heard you'd taken over operations on this spread and are hiring." Then, curiously, Jamey Dunn took a step back and struck a pose: weight propped on one hip, shoulders slouched, one long arm dangling at her side, opposite arm bent and thumb hooked in her belt loop. The caption under her could have read "Cowboy." The stance even had the right amount of loose-jointedness. It was a bid to make her seem even more masculine.

That's when Kell really got confused. He'd put out the word two days ago that he needed a cook/housekeeper, right after Uncle Bud's cook, Harvey Sample, left. Though by his own claim he wasn't a rancher, Harvey had held the ranch together until Kell got his affairs in order and could move to Plum Creek permanently. Kell had hoped Harvey would stay on, but Harvey guessed Kell would do better starting with another "youngun" like himself.

From what Kell could tell, Jamey Dunn certainly fit that requirement. And it wasn't that he would consider only a man for the job. But why would she deliberately try to appear more masculine?

He eyed her dubiously. "Yes, I'm hiring," he finally allowed.

"Then I'm here to apply for the job," she said in her husky voice.

"I see." Kell chewed the side of his lip and decided to be honest. "Forgive me if I'm a bit skeptical, Jamey. You're just about opposite of..."

His voice trailed off as he saw how his words made her expressive mouth stiffen in discouragement. Yet she set her jaw and said, "I've driven across three states to get here, Mr. Hamilton. I'd appreciate the opportunity to come in and talk to you, if I could, sir."

Despite his misgivings, he couldn't have ignored the desperation in her tone. Besides, who knew? Jamey Dunn just might be the man—woman, that is—for the job.

He nodded and held the door open for her.

She'd brought a bit of the cold day with her and a faint scent that was all her own. As before, his physical response was involuntary, a distinct awareness of her femaleness. It died quickly, though, when she passed and he got a close-up of that hat. It really had outlived its usefulness, even in a culture where well-broken-in headgear was worth its weight in gold.

Kell spied his new black Stetson hat hanging on a peg near the door. He knew it made him look like a weekend wrangler. He wasn't, at least not completely, but it'd be a while—and a lot of hard work—before he'd break in both the Stetson and his new occupation as rancher.

He wondered just what kind of life Jamey Dunn had led that put the age on that hat.

"Would you like some coffee?" Kell asked as he led the way to his office at the end of the hall.

"Thanks, no, I'm nur...not much of a coffee drinker." She fired a quick look at him. "Sir."

Kell caught her stutter and chalked it up to the nervousness he'd sensed in her earlier. And the wariness. They were both beginning to make him uneasy because he wondered what she had to be nervous and wary about.

This sir stuff had to stop at the very least. "Call me Kell," he advised, gesturing her into a chair.

Her eyes darting about her, she took a seat. She looked about as comfortable as a cat up a tree.

He gave a glance of his own around and saw this office, for the first time, from a woman's point of view. The house was rather rustic and could have used a good dusting and vacuuming. However mean a kidney stew Harvey made, he'd never won awards for his cleaning. Kell decided he wouldn't mind a woman's touch and attention to detail.

But he was at a loss as to how to put this woman at ease. Wasn't there some unstated rule about taking your hat off indoors? Or was that just men? Or just men's hats?

Kell asked, "A glass of water, maybe?"

"Water'd be fine," Jamey said, not calling him sir but not calling him Kell, either, as if she were humoring him.

Well, he needed humoring right now, because this whole situation was plain old weird. Something strange was going on with Jamey Dunn.

"I'll be back in a minute," he said, and gave the hat a pointed glance. "Make yourself at home. Please."

He returned to the kitchen and filled a glass with cold water. He suspected inviting her in for an interview was a mistake. Even if the woman had the skills needed for the position, she didn't seem to have the demeanor.

Well, maybe Jamey Dunn struck a different kind of relationship with the men she worked with. A just-one-of-the-boys camaraderie, as Harvey had.

But despite hat, boots and so on, Kell couldn't quite picture Jamey Dunn as one of the boys.

He rounded the corner to the office doorway and stopped dead, for Jamey had apparently heeded his unspoken suggestion and had shed her hat and gloves. He watched as she seemed to hesitate, then stood to shrug out of her coat, as well. Her back to the door, she put a hand to her spine and arched it, stretching the kinks out of the most curvaceous torso Kell had ever seen.

One of the boys, she was not.

A long red braid that must have been tucked inside her jacket hung down her back. Faded denim hugged her hips and thighs, and he comprehended just how long her legs were. Basically, they went halfway into tomorrow. She turned, and he got an unobstructed side view. Jamey Dunn was stacked.

His reaction was purely a gut one, as it had been seeing her walk, catching her scent. For propriety's sake, Kell battled it like before. However, he was very glad his male instincts were in full working order.

He caught her gaze. Her eyes were gray-green under auburn brows. Wisps of hair framed her face, which was dusted by a sprinkling of freckles. Now that he had the whole picture, Kell could see that Jamey Dunn was really very pretty. And not more than twenty years old.

Was that why she'd hidden her real appearance? Because he could see how she might consider her age a drawback in getting a cooking and housekeeping job on a ranch. There were a lot of experienced people out there looking for steady work.

Then he noticed that she was blushing. She seemed even younger, even more inexperienced. And alone. She'd come across three states to get here, she'd said.

Instead of responding with his glands this time, Kell felt an even deeper, more powerful tug on his insides, though he wasn't quite sure yet what it was.

Under his scrutiny, Jamey had hunched her shoulders and crossed her arms over her chest, trying still to hide her womanly attributes, and no wonder, the way he was staring at her. Kell checked his wandering gaze and pinned it firmly on her own with strict orders to stay put.

"Here's that water." He came into the room and handed the glass to her before settling into his chair behind the desk. She followed his lead and sat, too. Her gaze diligently avoided his, probably so she wouldn't have to deal with another instance of catching him eyeing her like a fox would a plump hen.

He did allow himself one last observation: she had the longest lashes.

"Well, where do you want to start?" he asked. "With your experience and qualifications?"

"Actually, I'd like to know a bit about the operation, if you don't mind."

He didn't, but he wondered at her interest in how the ranch was run, which had little to do with her job. "We're a large outfit, as far as spreads in the Panhandle go," Kell said. "Fifty sections. Near as I can tell so far, we're running about twenty-five to thirty head per section. Mostly Brangus, some Hereford, and the odd Brahman or longhorn. I won't know for sure what the count is till we do an inventory, which is going to take some time. The cows got pretty rangy over the past year, and a lot of fences are down."

"I'd heard the operation had gone downhill and the new owner was intending to try and make a go of it."

"My uncle left some capital for that," Kell asserted in Bud's defense. "And I've committed my own money to bringing this place up to spec as soon as possible. I'm making an all-out effort to get the repairs done on the outbuildings and fences right away. I've got a grand total of one source of live water on the place, so we've got to get the windmills in working order, which is essential, especially this time of year."

He paused as it occurred to him that he was doing a lot of explaining, above and beyond Jamey's questions. It was because he knew at some point he'd have to reveal that he was more than just new to Plum Creek Ranch. And for some reason, he wasn't sure that he wanted to reveal that piece of information.

"Are you sayin' you inherited this place?" Jamey asked.

"Yes. From my uncle, Bud Hamilton. He'd ranched in the Panhandle for fifty years," Kell said with more than a little pride. "Plum Creek's never been a gold mine, but it really only started having solvency problems when he got sick. And in the four months since he died."

"Then you've never ranched before in your life," she said, hitting the nail on the head. Did it show that much?

"I spent many a summer working here," Kell said, noting that he sounded a shade defensive. Damn, if he wasn't turning hot around the collar. "I learned a lot from Bud. And I've got a neighbor who's agreed to advise me in some of the finer aspects of day-to-day ranching. But I'm betting there's more to ranching than mending fence and riding cattle. There's the business side, and ranching is a business. I do have that kind of experience. Managing investments was my career in Dallas."

"Ranching isn't just any business," Jamey said, blunt as you please. Up to now she'd been pretty subdued, though something told him that wasn't her normal temperament. "There's more to it, just as you said. A lot more. It sure isn't just a job. You don't stand a chance of makin' it if that's how you see it."

Young she might be, but Jamey Dunn was not dull-witted. "You're right," Kell answered her honestly. "I don't see Plum Creek as 'just' a business. If I did, I wouldn't be here, because as investments go, this prospect is as risky as they come."

She seemed to digest his statement, the inside of her lower lip rubbing up and down over her upper one in a way that was a good deal distracting. "Why'd he leave Plum Creek to you?'' she asked after a few moments. She seemed intent, as if a lot rested on his answer. ''Your uncle, I mean.''

Again he wondered at the tack her interest had taken. ''I like to think it was because he considered me the one person in the family who gave a hoot about it, who might not sell it right off the bat. I aim to honor his faith in me,'' he said with a no-brag-just-fact intonation that anyone who knew his uncle would have pegged as Bud Hamilton's. He almost believed himself.

At that, her gaze mellowed, gray-green eyes reminding him of the sage that dotted the unforgiving terrain of the Panhandle. Somehow he felt he'd elevated his stature in her eyes, and he liked the sensation.

Then Jamey nodded. ''I can help you do that.''

''Maybe so.'' Kell leaned back in the rickety banker's chair and laced his fingers over his belt buckle. ''Why don't you tell me about your qualifications.''

She set her glass on the desk, sat tall, and cleared her throat like a school kid getting ready to recite. ''Well, I grew up on my daddy's ranch in Nevada. It wasn't as big as Plum Creek, just a two-man outfit, but I was one of those men, ever since I could sit a horse.''

''Beg pardon?'' What had sitting a horse to do with being a cook/housekeeper?

''I'm sayin' I can ride better than I can walk. I've done just about every kind of job a cowboy could do, worked cattle all my life. I can rope, wrestle, brand and steer 'em.''

He stared at her, struck dumb by the incongruity between what was coming out of her mouth and what he'd expected to hear. She was talking about castrating calves when he'd been thinking prize-winning, son-of-a-gun stew.

His silence seem to fluster her, for she rushed on. ''I'm not the least bit squeamish. I'm never sick.'' Her gaze flicked away at that, then streaked back again, earnest and intent. ''And I'm strong as they come, if I do say so myself. I'm good at line ridin'. I've even got my own stock saddle, and I can handle a gun, if the need ever comes up."

Kell listened to her catalog of skills with a growing sense of the peculiar. It dawned on him that this woman didn't want the job he doubted she was right for. She wanted the job he couldn't imagine she'd be right for. He didn't think he was out in left field with this conclusion, either; she'd obviously perceived the same problems as he had in her doing the job. Why else would she have tried to camouflage her femininity?

"You want to be a ranch hand?" he asked, just to be sure.

Her brow puckered. "Why else do you think I'm here?"

"Well, I never figured it was because you fancied yourself the next Annie Oakley." It wasn't the most tactful thing he'd ever said—well, hell, she'd surprised him—and so Kell understood her reaction to it.

Her shoulders slumped in disbelief and utter despair, making him feel like he'd led her on. Then she set her mouth in determination as he'd seen her do before. "You think because I'm a woman I can't do the job."

"Now I didn't say that," he protested—a little too quickly even to his own ears. But, honestly, he wasn't sexist! Or was he? In Dallas he'd worked for years alongside women and never once considered any one of them less competent at her job than a man.

Cowboying, though, wasn't just any job.

"Nothing personal, Jamey, but wrangling's a tough line of work that'd take the snap out of a man's brim, much less a woman's. It requires real strength and endurance, years of experience, and a certain nature to be good at it." He got the uncomfortable feeling he was justifying again.

"I'm strong," she said, as if that were his only objection. Abruptly she sat forward, sliding her arm toward him across the desktop, and lifted her forearm perpendicular to the surface. Her palm cupped slightly with her thumb cocked outward, her gaze intent on his, she issued the challenge.

"Don't be ridiculous." She may be one strapping woman, but he was no ninety-eight-pound weakling. There couldn't be any way she thought she'd succeed in beating him at arm wrestling. She simply didn't have what it would take to defeat him.

He started to get angry with her for having such unreasonable expectations—in wanting a job cowpunching and in challenging him so rashly. Then he peered into those gray-green eyes and again saw the stronger than ever desperation, her fear of not even getting a chance to prove herself, and it seemed a mirror of his own self-concerns. A defense, of sorts, of his own unlikely prospects and impractical aspirations.

Wondering what kind of fool he was, Kell sighed and leaned forward to grasp her smaller hand in his. A ready-set-go count and the match was on.

She *was* strong. He felt his biceps strain against the power of hers, though still not with any threat of being overcome. His respiration remained steady even after two minutes had passed. Jamey, in the meantime, had grown progressively redder, starting at her neckline and finally reaching her cheeks. He was actually wondering how long he should resist her, proving his point, before calling this off, when she bit her lip against an insuppressible half pant, half groan of effort. And it put him in mind of a different kind of physical activity—a different kind of match.

A stirring started way down in Kell's gut. Of its own volition, his gaze slid downward. With unerring accuracy it zeroed in on Jamey's shirtfront where strained one little button, the one right between her breasts, and it looked like it was fixing to pop with her next breath.

The back of his hand came to within an inch of touching the desktop. He jerked his gaze back to hers, saw she knew where it had strayed. It was as if a chemical reaction went off between them. A rush of competitive adrenaline, mixed with something pure male in him, reacting to something pure female in her, launched their joined hands upright. And with what seemed like no effort, Kell pressed Jamey's forearm back and down, pinning it to the desktop, not painfully but with conviction.

Their fingers remained entwined, their gazes still locked. Yes, she was desperate, and it had spurred her to foolhardiness. He actually saw her realize her mistake. If she'd something to prove, she had picked the wrong method of argument. The discouragement crept back into her eyes.

As for himself, he felt ashamed for allowing his baser urges to rouse him to such a demonstration of might. For a moment he'd been predatory in a way that wouldn't be denied. His head even sang, as if he were under the influence of some drug, and maybe he was. It was the kind of drug that brought out a certain ingrained aggressiveness. And made him arm wrestle a woman, knowing she didn't have a chance.

He felt regret, too; the regard he'd sensed from her had surely died with his little show of plain old male domination.

Kell noticed that both of them still leaned toward one another across the desk, their noses six inches apart. Down curved her expressive mouth, which he'd already learned signaled her state of mind even more than her eyes. Then that mouth opened, said distinctly, "I can do the job," and Kell discovered what else she'd been hiding: Jamey Dunn had a stubborn streak to go along with that red hair.

"How old are you, Jamey?" he asked, figuring he'd broken every other rule of conducting a proper employment interview, he might as well shoot the whole ball of wax. In Dallas, the Equal Employment Opportunity Commission would have had his head on a china platter by now.

"Twenty-two," she answered.

"Twenty-two. Well, when I was that age, full of beans and stronger and stubborner than I'd ever been in my life, I couldn't even compete with my uncle, forty years older than me."

"But I'm one of the hardest workers you're likely to find—"

"That's my point. It isn't just hard work—"

"My daddy always said there's nothing can replace good old grit, and I've got grit!"

"Damn it, Jamey, don't you see?" Why on earth did he find it so important to convince this woman that he couldn't see her handling the job, when he should have ended this interview long ago with one simple statement? "It's not a matter of wanting to do it. It's not even so much a matter of strength or endurance. It's a matter of building up a real feel for cattle and horses and the land, and maybe having a sense for them that can't be learned. I mean, even I—"

Just in time, he clamped his mouth shut over his next words. *Even I have my doubts that I can handle the job.*

Reluctant for her to read his thoughts in his eyes, Kell rose and found something to look at out the window. It was the featureless, flat-as-a-griddle grassland of West Texas. Never real picturesque, the landscape was even more bleak in the winter with nary a tumbleweed to break the perspective. Bud Hamilton had lived most of his seventy-two years here, keeping this ranch going through scourges of biblical proportions, not to mention bottomed-out cattle markets. Yet Kell couldn't deny this land, this calling, had its appeal. One that had always seemed to draw him as he'd seen it capture and hold Bud like a lover. One that had now caused Kell to act perhaps with an even greater foolhardiness than Jamey Dunn ever could.

It was because some of the best times in Kell's life had been spent here. Since he was seven, it'd been like a three-month-long trip to the world's best summer camp, an escape from a place where his mother and father were no longer married to each other, where he wasn't convenient in their busy lives.

Here, he could forget those feelings, be one of the boys. The only thing that mattered was the land and doing their job well. Bud had been their boss, as well as the best of cowboys. "Could darn near think like a cow or a horse," the other men had often said with admiration.

The last of them had left when Bud died.

Yes, Bud Hamilton had taught his nephew, more than either of Kell's own parents, how to be a cowboy—no, how to be a man—in the best sense of the word. You didn't complain. You didn't shirk your work. You dealt with people fairly and honestly and you expected them to do the same. And you took responsibility for those who depended on you.

Kell shifted his feet, propping the heel of his hand on the window jamb as he continued to stare outside, to try and look at the situation objectively. He gave himself credit for being a fair hand; still, his roping, riding and cutting skills had grown pretty rusty in the ten years since the last summer he'd worked on the ranch. Yet, as he'd told Jamey, he did have a head for business, which would play a significant part in whether the ranch survived. That meant hiring the most competent, strongest hands money could buy. Until he found his own in his role as rancher, he had to let his cowboys take up the slack, and there was no shame in that.

That's what the logical side of him said. The other side of him, housing that tender male ego, was in the throes of an identity crisis he'd nearly been able to corral until now. Because he knew there were no assurances that even with experience he'd have what it took to be a rancher—or maybe the kind of rancher Bud had been, with a sixth sense about his land, cattle and men. It was one thing to struggle with this apprehension himself, but Kell wasn't sure how he felt about putting his doubt out there for the whole world—or was it just pretty Jamey Dunn?—to come and take a peck at it.

Kell turned. Jamey was perched on the edge of her chair, one hand clutching her knee, the other fisted and resting on the edge of the desk. She stared at the floor as if trying to master a few of her own demons. She really was something; a magnificent specimen of a woman. But he didn't see even hale and hearty Jamey Dunn being up to the kind of grueling work he expected out of his men, at least not as a full-time job. It was going to be hard enough to make a go of this ranch.

And above all, Plum Creek had to be his biggest priority.

Chapter Two

Kell returned to his chair behind the desk.

"Maybe if I explained the situation here at Plum Creek," he said. "You see, in order to maximize the ranch's productivity and stay on a tight budget, I needed to hire the best hands for the most reasonable pay—men with experience and endurance."

Jamey glanced up. "'Needed'?"

"I'm sorry, Jamey," he said gently. She looked incredibly vulnerable, and younger than her twenty-two years. "I filled the last of the hired hand positions four days ago."

She sat back in slow motion. "Why didn't you tell me that in the first place?"

"I apologize. I should have, but I simply wasn't thinking of hiring you in that capacity. I assumed you were looking for something else."

Granted, again his phrasing wasn't the best, but somehow he'd hit a real panic button with her. She popped out of her chair like a prairie dog up from its hole. Her cheeks reddened and she loomed over the desk as if trying to make herself more substantial. "Is that why you invited me in here?" she asked, her alto voice leaping an octave. "What'd you *think* I was looking for?"

Baffled, Kell put up a placating hand. "Hold on a minute."

Then he saw it. Not wariness, but stark fear.

Again he acted instinctively. He stood, hand still held up in appeasement, meaning to reassure her. She took a step back.

He sat down.

"I was thinking of you for the job of cook and housekeeper," he explained. "The position came open two days ago, and since I'd already hired all my cowboys and, well, since you are a woman, I guess I just assumed that's what brought you here."

Jamey digested his words. "Oh," she said in a small voice as she sank into her chair. She even flashed a quick, sheepish grin. It was the first real smile to reach her eyes, and the openness it brought to her face surprised him. She really was pretty. And young—much too young to be chasing across the Southwest in search of an uncertain future.

A thought hit him. "You said you were raised on your father's ranch."

The last vestiges of her smile disappeared. "I was."

"What happened to it?"

"It . . . it's gone," she said.

"And your father?"

She continued to look at him, but he knew it wasn't his face she saw.

"Gone," she repeated, and Kell shut up. Whether the ranch had been sold, foreclosed upon, or destroyed by any number of calamities, in Jamey's mind it was clearly as irretrievable as if it'd been on the moon. And her father . . . Kell spied the battered hat hanging on the back of her chair. He knew, suddenly, whose hat Jamey wore.

Kell felt a well of empathy spill over within him, and could have cursed himself. He wasn't just putty; he was putty in its genetic form. It didn't make good business sense, he argued against his impulse, hiring Jamey Dunn for any job on Plum Creek. But then, as she'd pointed out, he'd never succeed if all he considered was the business side of ranching. It was a way of life, where one's word was gold, where one offered to share a bit of bread and beans even when the pickings were slim.

For Kell, taking on this ranch was an attempt not only to become closer to the land, perhaps closer to the past, but more to become closer to himself. He wasn't some city slicker yearning to try cowboying—but if being a cowboy meant being more of a man.... Suddenly he knew his Uncle Bud would have taken Jamey in without a second thought.

Still he wondered at his next words even as he said them, "I can offer you the cook/housekeeper job, if you want it. The pay isn't as much as a hand's, but you'd have a lot more freedom. You get Sundays off and use of the ranch pickup when the boys are done with it to make supply runs into Borger."

"You mean it's a live-in position?" Jamey asked.

"They all are. There's a double-wide out back that houses the permanent hands, and an old, rundown bunkhouse that the short-termers are using."

"I see." She shifted uneasily. "I'd sort of hoped to keep my own quarters in town, if I was able to get hired on here."

Kell frowned. "It's not really practical. After all, Borger's fifty miles from Plum Creek. An awful long way, especially in bad weather. I guess that's why Plum Creek has always been a bachelor outfit, out of necessity. Single men without family attachments are more willing to put up with the isolation and long hours."

"That's not exactly the problem..." Again, Jamey crossed her arms protectively over her breasts.

It struck Kell then, the reason for her hesitation. "As cook and housekeeper, you'd have the private room and bathroom across the breezeway, totally separate from the main house," he explained, hoping to allay any apprehensions of him having designs on her, if that was why she'd reacted so radically to his previous slip of the tongue. "I know it's not the position you came here for, but it's steady work, and—" he studied her thoughtfully "—I get the impression you need a place to call home."

She sat in silence for a few moments. Then she said, "Can I ask you a question?"

"Shoot."

"If one of those cowhand positions had been open, would you've given me a chance to prove myself at it?"

He tugged on his earlobe. Putting her in the kitchen was one thing, putting her out with the boys was an entirely different situation. There were bound to be some complications arising from daily dangling this buxom thing in front of the bunch of rather rough and rugged—not to mention sex-deprived—wranglers he'd hired. Look at the rise she got out of him, and Kell considered himself above that sort of reaction. Though he had yet to learn the personalities of his hands, their strengths and weaknesses, just as he had yet to learn his own, letting Jamey ride with the boys was out of the question.

That concluded, Kell answered, "I don't . . . know."

"I see." She thought some more. "I guess the fair thing would be to tell you I'm not swift with an oven or a dust rag."

"How long could it take to brush up on your skills? You said you were a hard worker. I'd like to give you a chance to prove that, Jamey." He realized he'd made her an offer because he wanted his own assurance that experience or innate talent weren't the deciding factors in one's success.

Now it was her turn to rise, take the few steps over to the window and stare out of it. "You said you weren't goin' to sell the ranch right away. But would you sell it later, once you got it profitable?''

"The more likely event would be having to give it up if I can't get it into the black. But to answer your question, no. Plum Creek is my home. It's my livelihood and my career now." It was the first time he'd said those words aloud, and Kell meant them. Perhaps that was why doubts assailed him. There was no turning back now. It was either succeed or fail in the most clear-cut of terms.

He noticed that her gaze had returned to his and once more he saw her considering him. Evaluating. Judging.

"I accept your offer," Jamey said formally. "I mean to show you I can do the job." She shifted onto one hip as she slid her fingers into her back pockets. The stance was again a masculine one, yet Kell got the idea it wasn't a calculated posture so much as a look at the real Jamey Dunn. The position, however, thrust her full breasts against her shirt-front. Kell got a tactile impression of her palms pressing against her backside, as if his own hands rested there, of her chest up against his. The physical effect on him was again swift and definite.

He shifted in his chair and shook his head. He'd have to keep rein on such thoughts and impulses, and make it clear to the boys that, while it wasn't a crime to be attracted to a pretty woman, he wouldn't tolerate any disrespect of her.

"Then welcome to Plum Creek," he said, standing. His immediate inclination was to shake on the deal, but he remembered the feel of her gloved hand in his, and the result, and decided it better to forgo the convention.

Yet, Jamey, after an instant of hesitation—as if she were reminding herself of something, too—stepped forward and extended her right hand. "I won't let you down...Kell."

He tried to ignore the feel of her fingers, callused as a man's yet fine-boned as only a woman's could be, tried to ignore the husky way she said his name, how it looked coming from those full lips. He really did. But Kell didn't have to wonder this time why the wariness returned to her eyes.

And the sudden doubt that maybe she'd made a mistake, too.

Jamey Dunn stealthily opened the door marked 19 at the Route 152 Inn and entered the motel room. All was quiet in the darkened interior. Head back and eyes closed, Glenna Dunn sat with the cast on her left ankle propped on the edge of the bed.

Jamey glanced around in sudden anxiety before she noticed the blanket-covered form on the bed. She felt a prick of disappointment to go along with the discomfort she'd endured for the past hour, then decided it was probably for the best, as they both could use the sleep.

Leaning against the door, she chided herself for her jumpiness. Yet the racing of her heart was not a result of the imagined alarm a moment ago.

What had she done?

Glenna opened her eyes. "You're back," she said. "I started to worry when you were gone so long, then figured you wouldn't've been kept if the news was bad." She squinted at her daughter in the obscure light. "Is it?"

Without answering, Jamey pushed off from the door and crossed the room to her mother's side, tugging at the waistband on her jeans. Today was the first time she'd worn this pair in several months and they'd started cutting into her side five minutes after she'd put them on. She didn't consider herself overweight, was really only five pounds heavier than she'd been a year ago, but her body dimensions had shifted. She had the feeling that while she might eventually lose an inch here or there, her skinny tomboy days, among other things, were gone for good.

"How's the new cast feelin' now that you've had a chance to put your leg up?" she whispered to her mother.

"I don't have the faintest notion how the cast feels," Glenna said drolly, her own voice soft of a silent accord. "My ankle, on the other hand, itches to beat the band. The swelling's gone down some, though." She set her foot on the floor and started to rise. Jamey's hand shot out to support Glenna under her elbow. The older woman waved her away. "Shoo. I'm not an invalid."

Jamey withdrew her hand. "I never thought you were, Momma. I just hate to see you struggling when I can help."

Glenna's gray eyes softened as she stood awkwardly. "I know, sugar. Sorry I'm so cranky. But bein' laid up with this broken ankle makes me feel older than Methuselah."

"Forty-one's not old," Jamey protested quickly. On the contrary, Glenna Dunn could have passed for Jamey's older sister. Though much slighter than Jamey, Glenna normally had the energy of the younger woman, as well. That's how she'd broken her ankle, taking on what should have been her daughter's responsibility, Jamey thought with another pang. Yet she knew the broken ankle wasn't the main reason her mother had been feeling old of late.

She turned away, shed her coat and hat rather than watch her mother stump to the wall heater, which was making a high-pitched rattle. Glenna fiddled with the thermostat. "Pathetic thing. It has two settings—broilin' hot or freezin' cold, which isn't good for any of us. I hope we won't have to stay here long."

"We won't," Jamey said. "That's what took me so long. I found an apartment in town, partly furnished. Ground floor so you won't have to climb stairs."

Glenna turned. "You got the job then?"

"No. The ranch hand positions were filled a few days ago."

"Aw, sugar, I'm sorry. I know you were hoping, with the new owner hiring a fresh crew, that you'd have a better chance of getting on at this ranch than the others that turned you down. And we were too late!"

"Yes, well ... I did get *a* job."

"*A* job?" Glenna echoed. "Doing what?"

Jamey gave her mother the determined look she'd given Kell Hamilton. "I'm the new cook and housekeeper for the Plum Creek outfit."

Her mother said nothing, just braced an elbow on the back of the wrist resting against her middle. Her index finger pressed against her lips as if to hold back her words.

Jamey had often thought over the past year that things would be a lot easier if her mother came out with whatever she was thinking. But that had never been Glenna's way. Besides, just as often, mostly in the darkness when she lay in bed for hour after sleepless hour, Jamey was glad to leave the unsaid unsaid. She had a secret hope that if they avoided certain subjects, then perhaps she could right the situation before ever acknowledging that things had gone wrong. And that it was her fault they had. She knew that Glenna had her own need to make amends, but Jamey was even less ready to serve as confessor, again because, in her mind, the final chapter on everyone's guilt had yet to be written.

"I know I've never been good around the house," she said, forestalling a similar comment by her mother. "But I never really put my mind to it. And as for that waitressing job I got fired from—" she rushed on, again attempting to avoid another point Glenna might bring up "—I'll be the first to admit I probably never would've gotten the hang of it. But that wasn't real kitchen work. No creativity at all. Now, the actual act of cooking—*there's* a challenge. I'm looking forward to it."

Glenna lifted an auburn brow. "Doesn't sound like it's *me* you're trying to convince."

"I can do the job," Jamey said, just as she had to Kell. "I won't fail." Her husky voice, never steady, broke on that last word, perhaps because she'd cut off the one she couldn't say. *I won't fail—again.*

"You haven't failed, Jamey," her mother said gently, accurately reading her daughter's fear, anyway.

Jamey neither agreed nor disagreed. To do so would have started the stampede, more words she wasn't ready to face, yet. Once again she had an overwhelming urge to go to the bed and its occupant, to seek unconditional acceptance from the one being on earth she could, right now.

Instead, she stooped to investigate the contents of a battered foam cooler. She hadn't had lunch, didn't feel much like it, but she needed to keep her liquids up, at least. Floating in the cold water was a container of juice. She unscrewed the cap and took a swallow.

Studying the label on the bottle without really seeing it, she said, "I'll... I'll need your help, Momma. I told the owner I'd start day after tomorrow. The cleaning I think I'll be able to handle on my own, but the cookin'...."

"I'll help you any way I can, sugar. You know that."

Jamey did. She shifted her shoulders, trying to relieve the increasing pressure in her chest.

"I'll admit," Glenna added, "I'm somewhat relieved you didn't get work wrangling so soon after—"

"It's been three months," Jamey interrupted. "It's time."

"Still, you didn't have to take this job, you know," Glenna ventured, stating what Jamey hadn't allowed herself to consider. "Just because we drove so far. I've told you there's no rush. We've still got some money from the ranch sale and your father's life insurance to last a while."

"That's your money, Momma, your old age fund."

"Which is a good bit in the future," Glenna said tartly. "But some of it's yours, too. Even though your daddy didn't have a will, I know he'd've wanted you to have part of this money. I don't intend to live on it till it's gone, myself. As soon as this cast comes off, I'll need to be out earning a living, too." She glanced toward the bed. "Maybe once I'm better again, I can take over the job at Plum Creek for you, and you'll be able to—"

"Do the job there I'm best trained for," Jamey finished for her. *The only job I'm trained for—anywhere.* "That's what I was thinkin' myself."

Glenna frowned. "You said the hand positions were filled."

"They are. But the owner of Plum Creek is new to ranching. I figured I could show him I'm a hard worker, maybe help him and the other hands out, and he'd see that I know what I'm doin'. When one of the hired hand spots comes up for grabs, I'll be there to fill the position. And I'll even be able to bring in my replacement. You."

"I see," Glenna mused. "Plum Creek's owner, whatever his name is—"

"Kell Hamilton," Jamey said, her gaze faltering.

"Mr. Hamilton. Does he know you're inexperienced as a cook?"

"He knows." Another falter.

"He must be new to ranchin', all right."

"Momma, I'm not tryin' to pull anything over on him." She thought of certain . . . details she'd omitted telling Kell. But they wouldn't affect her ability to do her job. "I feel I have a chance to prove myself at Plum Creek. Kell seemed different from the ranchers who turned me down without so much as a by-your-leave." The indignity of those encounters was still fresh, but had given her a picture of the attitude she'd been sheltered from most of her life. And what she was up against. "You know Daddy always said a body could do whatever he—or she—put their mind to. Kell struck me as believing that. He's at Plum Creek to make a go of ranching. Maybe because of that he seemed willin' to believe in me, too."

Jamey thought back over her interview. No, Kell Hamilton wasn't a typical rancher. If he had been, he'd have told her no way on God's earth would he hire her, just as the others had, even without knowing the particulars about her. It was one thing for a woman to help men run a ranch; it was an entirely different matter for her to bill herself out as a top-notch hand.

Nevertheless, Jamey knew she was a darned good cowgirl. She'd been taught by the best. James Dunn had run his small but respectable ranch almost single-handedly. He could do it all.

No, not all, she amended with a familiar stab of regret. She'd realized this only after leaving home. Only after returning to try to run it by herself. And failing.

Again, Jamey shot an urgent glance at the bed. *Please, wake up.* She resisted the urge to literally yank on the front of her shirt in physical distress.

Instead, she forced another gulp of juice past the lump in her throat. She realized she wanted, very much, to see Kell Hamilton succeed, to help him succeed—and it was because she saw her opportunity to make up for one of the mistakes she'd made. To atone for the heartache she'd caused. To save something similar to what was forever lost to her and her mother.

"Kell Hamilton," she reflected, "seems a lot like Daddy."

"But, sugar..." Glenna hesitated, then said softly, "That's what you thought about Henry McSween."

Jamey flushed. "I didn't mean.... For sure, Henry could ride and rope as good as any cowboy," she admitted. "But I didn't mean Kell was like Daddy that way. I don't know if he could bust a calf if his life depended on it. I meant he seemed fair."

"I see," Glenna said, and Jamey wondered if her mother did see or if it was one of those buried issues that needed to be exhumed before it could truly be laid to rest.

Kell *had* seemed fair. And open-minded. Not at all your regular cowboy—except for during their little arm wrestle. That had been her error in judgment, though, drawing a line and not expecting a cowboy to step over it. Something in a man's genes made him act that way. *Or jeans,* she thought ruefully.

After Henry, she should know better. But she'd been so desperate, she just couldn't think of anything else to do to keep Kell from showing her the door then and there.

"Well," Glenna said, "regardless of the job you hope for, you're going to have to hang on to this one to get a stab at it."

Jamey nodded. "I thought tonight we'd move into the apartment. I'll unload the trailer while you write down recipes. Then we'll make lists of supplies both of us'll need, and shop tomorrow. I'll be able to keep you in groceries when I come into town every few days." She noticed the dawning concern on her mother's face, and added quickly, "Of course, you'll have the pickup if an emergency comes up, but I aim for you not to have to drive till that ankle heals unless it's unavoidable."

"But won't you need the truck?"

"I'll have the ranch pickup," she explained.

Her mother still looked puzzled. "Mr. Hamilton'll let you keep it here every night?"

"No...just on Saturday nights and Sundays, my day off." There was no putting it off any longer. Jamey looked her mother in the eye. "It's a live-in position."

"Oh, Jamey." Glenna's voice filled with dismay. And disappointment, whether with, for, or in her daughter, Jamey couldn't tell. She could guess. "How can you live away from—"

"I don't have a choice. We talked of having to do this if I got a ranch job."

"But only as a last resort."

"This *is* my last resort." Jamey swallowed back that infernal lump making her voice even more hoarse. "I need a job doin' what I know how to do. This seemed the closest I was going to get."

The impact of the morning's events and the course she'd chosen hit her fully, bringing a sting to her eyes. She turned away, blinking rapidly. It seemed the words of regret and self-doubt were going to come out despite her efforts to suppress them, because right now her heart was as full as it could stand to be. "I suppose I could've waited for another prospect to turn up, but God knows when or where it'd be. I just couldn't wait anymore, Momma. I had to make a decision. It's past time for me to take charge of my life and get to work. I need to care for you—"

"Sugar, I told you that's not your job."

"It should be, then. It's my fault you're laid up like this, with no place to call home."

"Lord, you're stubborn!" Glenna declared. "I'll tell you who's the spitting image of James Dunn."

"That may be," Jamey snapped, then said more softly, "That very well may be, and it means I must take care of my responsibilities, take care of you. Take care of Hettie—"

A quavering wail came from the lump on the bed. It snuffled and rooted around, then emitted another cry, one tinged with the fear of isolation.

Jamey moved to the bed and scooped up the bundle, tucking it into the crook of her arm.

"Hush now, sugar bump. Momma's here." She pushed back the blanket and drank in the vision of a red, screwed-up face and bald head. Her daughter, Hettie. Henrietta McSween, named for her daddy as Jamey had been named for hers. Despite all that had happened, the losses, the heartache, the disillusionments on all sides, she still considered the birth of her daughter a blessing that she would never, ever regret. And it made her cherish the secret hope that everything she'd done in the past year hadn't been a mistake, but part of some grand plan she just didn't have the whole picture for, yet.

The whimpers changed in nature. A tiny cheek pressed insistently against her breast, seeking. Jamey undid the buttons on her shirt one-handedly and unclasped the opening on her nursing bra. The small mouth found her nipple with faultless accuracy, pulling on it greedily, painfully.

Jamey didn't mind. With a relief that was more emotional than physical, she felt the pressure in her chest ease. She glanced up and met her mother's eyes.

"Does Kell know about Hettie?" Glenna asked.

"Momma," Jamey said, feeling suddenly weary beyond her years. "Henry doesn't even know about Hettie."

Glenna, once again, said nothing. But between mother and daughter remained all the unstated, unexpressed words. And more.

Chapter Three

Tonight was going to be one of those nights when sleep eluded Jamey. The lumpy mattress on the fold-out couch didn't help. Nor did the unfamiliar sounds of the small apartment.

She concentrated, listening, and distinguished the reassuring sound of her mother's soft breathing. Then she listened harder, even raised her head off the pillow. Finally she rose and padded into the single bedroom. She knelt and peered through the mesh side of the playpen next to Glenna's bed.

And Jamey located the sound she'd needed to hear.

The baby lay on a quilted pad. Tomorrow Jamey would assemble Hettie's crib and set up her mobiles. Tonight, though, Jamey wondered if the pen was too cold for the baby, this close to the floor. She lay down on the thinly carpeted surface and decided it was. Rising, she lifted her daughter, blankets and all, and carried her to the sofa bed. Trying not to jostle Hettie awake, Jamey made a nest, settled the baby into it, and curled around it and her daughter.

Hettie awoke anyway, though she didn't cry. Dimly, Jamey saw a doughnut-shaped mouth through which the tip of a tongue poked in and out. Her dark eyes shone, avid and darting about. Hettie was listening hard, too.

"Hey, sugar bump," Jamey whispered, and Hettie turned her head toward the sound. Her small fists, tucked against her chest, clenched in recognition.

Jamey touched her lips to the downy forehead, then brushed them back and forth. She pulled back to see Hettie's reaction. The baby blinked and kicked her feet. *More,* she seemed to say. Jamey stroked a finger down her velvety cheek and was rewarded with the squint of one eye as Hettie opened her mouth, turning eagerly toward the touch.

"You can't be hungry again," Jamey muttered.

Hettie gave an impatient kick. And a warning mewl.

Jamey sighed and unbuttoned the front of her pajamas. She nestled the baby closer as Hettie found her target, first try.

Actually, she didn't mind nursing the child. She craved the contact with Hettie, in fact; the connection only they shared. But she should try to wean the little one, as much as she could in a day's time. After tomorrow, Hettie would go on the bottle exclusively.

Jamey didn't want to think about it.

The baby gazed up at her as the little mouth worked like a suction pump. At three months, Hettie seemed pretty certain to have brown eyes. Her hair would be red, if the copper dusting on Hettie's skull was any gauge. Jamey hoped her daughter would be as red-headed as a bantam rooster, as James Dunn had been.

Henry McSween's hair was brown. So were his eyes—a sparkly, roguish brown that could coax and cajole, making words of the same kind virtually unnecessary. He was a smooth talker, all the same. She could see how a different kind of woman might not have held out long enough to get a ring on her finger before giving in to that man and his charming ways. In a way, it probably would have been better if she had been that kind of woman, Jamey thought, not for the first time.

Did you really think it'd last forever? That's what Henry had said the night before he'd left her.

Yes, I did! she'd wanted to shout at him. She would never have married him if she hadn't believed it was possible to do whatever she'd set her mind to doing.

Yet the words had brought her down to earth with a crash. "It" was their marriage, not some trashy affair as he'd made it sound, and his question an answer to hers. Fed up with weeks of neglect and hurting inside, she'd asked him what kind of life and marriage he'd intended for them.

Jamey shifted, trying to find an un-lumpy area to rest her backside. Hettie had dozed off before she'd barely started nursing. The nipple had popped out of her mouth, her eyes half closed and crossed in satiated, stupefied slumber. Jamey had seen the expression before. No, Hettie hadn't been hungry, just looking for a pacifier to help put her back to sleep.

She'd definitely have some of her father's traits besides his brown eyes.

Kell Hamilton also had brown eyes. Yet they were different from Henry's, not so much in color as expression. While Henry's had sparkled, Kell's glowed, liquid and warm. She'd liked, too much, the way he'd gazed at her, quiet and thoughtful-like—except for the times when she'd caught him looking at her with a deeper glow, a . . . smoldering, like a banked fire that belied the intensity of the heat radiating within it.

Reflexively, Jamey pressed Hettie closer to her breast. Maybe she *was* that kind of woman. Or just that kind when it came to cowboys. Kell Hamilton didn't seem like a regular cowboy, though, even if her acquaintance with "regu-

lar'' cowboys could only be called sketchy. Sure, he looked
natural—and fine—in snug-fitting jeans and a Western-style
shirt with a hint of dark hair showing at his open collar.
She'd seen the way his biceps had strained against that material. He certainly seemed rugged as a cowboy: broad-
shouldered and solid-looking in a way that wouldn't be
blown away by the blustery winds sweeping across the
plains. And tall. Kell Hamilton was tall.

There weren't many men Jamey had to look up to.

But then, there were his Saturday night boots with not a
scuff on them. And that haircut she'd never seen on a man
walking out of a country barber shop. Even when Kell had
run his fingers through the medium-brown strands, they'd
still fallen back into place perfectly. Well, maybe not so
perfectly. Some of them fell over his forehead in a fascinating disarray. But *doggone* if it still didn't seem styled to look
that way.

So she was attracted to Kell Hamilton, and he was attracted to her. It didn't mean anything—heaven knew she'd
learned that, if nothing else. In fact, it was better this way,
knowing from the first that, even if Kell wasn't the same
kind of cowboy Henry had been, he sure looked at her the
same way Henry had, and men were men, no matter what.
By no means was it going to stop her from working for him.
She had meant what she'd said when she'd told her mother
she wanted to help Kell Hamilton succeed.

To be honest with herself, though, she did have a somewhat selfish motive in mind for taking the cook position at
Kell's ranch. This was her best chance to get a job not only
that she was good at, but to be someone she could believe in
again. She'd been a failure as a daughter and wife. As a
mother...she couldn't bear considering that she might fail
Hettie. Jamey knew she had to start now to become the
parent Hettie would respect and look up to, the kind of
person Jamey felt was worth looking up to. She didn't know
any other way to do it than by being a cowgirl. She'd long

ago given up the idea she could be whatever she wanted to be.

On that thought, another question echoed in her head. Her question, asked of her father the day she'd brought Henry McSween—her husband—home.

"Daddy, he's a bang-up cowboy, best I've ever seen. Good as you. Doesn't that count for somethin'?"

"Bein' good at a certain thing don't mean you're automatically cut out for another," he'd said, looking a decade older than his forty-one years. "Doin' what comes...naturally to a person might seem right 'cause you can do it practically without thinkin'. But it don't make it good."

Her head had reeled in confusion. What was he saying? Did he mean *she* wasn't a good cowboy? Or maybe she was, but that was all he saw her being.

At a loss, Jamey had fallen back on her training: to take responsibility for her actions.

"I'm goin' with Henry," she'd said. She had looked up at her father, six-foot-five and solid as a tree, yet trembling with regret and disappointment and hurt. Well, she'd been disappointed and hurt, too. He'd *told* her she was capable. "You always said I could do whatever I wanted to do in this world."

"That I did, daughter," he'd said, eyes pained as he regarded her for what would be the last time in either of their lives. "It's what the world will do to you I can't control."

The night was at its deepest, Jamey noticed as she came out of her recollection.

It hadn't taken her long, a mere three months, to realize the mistake she'd made marrying Henry McSween. Her father had seen from the first she wasn't cut out for being a wife. So when she had failed at it, she'd started not to believe in herself or her judgment. The only thing she could think of to do was to try to erase the mistake she'd made and return to some semblance of her old life. Jamey had caught a bus to Reno, gotten a quickie divorce to end her quickie marriage, and continued on down the road home. She'd even taken back her maiden name, as if the marriage had never happened.

Except two days later she'd discovered she was pregnant. Two days after that, her father had died.

Not bothering to rebutton the front of her nightgown, Jamey cuddled her daughter next to her skin. Three months ago she'd looked into her newborn child's face and had gotten an idea of what her father had meant in their last conversation. Though Jamey had become a mother, it wasn't a role she fit into naturally. And she was terrified she never would.

She knew of no way to proceed, though, except to try to instill in her daughter the rules she'd been raised with and still believed were the best: you dealt with people fairly and honestly and you expected them to do the same. You worked hard. And you took responsibility for your actions.

For your mistakes.

Jamey knew she would have to tell Kell about Hettie, should have told him today, but something very like maternal protectiveness had kicked in. She needed the housekeeping job, needed the wrangler job, and if Kell had his doubts she could handle it as a woman, he'd be sure to see her in an even less feasible light knowing she was a mother.

Yes, she was a mother, and that was a role she couldn't run away from, a fact she couldn't change, even if she'd wanted to.

Jamey wedged the tip of her finger into Hettie's tiny fist. Even in sleep, the child clung to the digit. Tomorrow she'd leave her baby, and the thought of it made Jamey want to die. She felt caught in a trap, almost like having to give up her daughter to keep her. Even knowing Hettie would be in good hands with Glenna, Jamey found herself searching her mind for another solution. Henry? He didn't know about his daughter, but Jamey knew someday she would have to

find him and tell him. He had a right to know. He was her
father, and despite everything, Jamey wanted her daughter
to know her daddy was a cowboy. For now, though, the
most she was willing to give Henry of his daughter was his
name. She wanted her chance to put things right, a chance
to provide for her child, to do what was best. To do *her* best.

But how could it be best for her to be away from her little
girl day and night, even temporarily?

Jamey tried to sniff back her tears, but they came, anyway, one after another. She pressed her face into the crook
of Hettie's neck. Jamey knew, however, even if she was able
to muffle her crying, her mother would know in the morning. Again, neither would say anything.

Kell awoke in heaven—if heaven smelled like fresh-brewed
coffee on a brisk January morning.

Ten minutes later, shaved and dressed, he entered the
kitchen and located the source of his newfound ideology in
an old-fashioned metal pot that he had seen Harvey use. Its
innards had confounded Kell, and since he'd somehow believed it cheating to buy an automatic drip machine, he'd
been drinking instant for the past four days, which was certainly hell in anyone's book. He poured himself a cup and
took a tongue-scorching sip. Yup. Sheer heaven.

He glanced around and saw that a pile of silverware and
a stack of plates had been dumped on the trestle table, where
sat a crockery pitcher of orange juice and a brick of butter
on a saucer. The smell of sausage was just starting to ema-
nate from a covered skillet sizzling on the back burner of the
stove. On the counter, amid a disaster of spilled flour,
splatters of cooking oil and eggshells, rested a bowl of what
looked like pancake batter. So far, so good, he thought, and
had begun to congratulate himself on doing a decent job
hiring Jamey when he heard murmuring down the hall and
stuck his head around the corner. Jamey, her back toward

him, bent over the telephone table as she scribbled on a pad of paper.

"Uh-huh," she said. "What's hot enough…? A drop of water *dances* on it? Okay, whatever you say. How many? I forget…*double* the recipe? How in tarnation do you double a recipe?" Jamey shifted, planting her weight on one leg, which thrust her hip out and put the denim she wore through the kind of stress Kell bet Levi Strauss had never tested.

Yup, he thought.

"What was that?" Jamey said, and Kell's stomach did a flip as he realized he leaned through the doorway at close to a forty-five-degree angle. He quickly backed into the kitchen and had a seat at the table.

Yet she didn't seem to have heard him in the background, and he could still hear her conversation. "Hungry?" she said with dismay. "But it's only five o'clock! No, I'll let you go. I—I'll manage. Will you, though?" Her voice turned to pure misery. "It's just that it doesn't sound like only hunger to me…all right, I'll call you later."

Kell heard the sound of the phone being returned to its cradle and glanced around for something to make it look as if he hadn't overheard. He swept up a handful of forks and began setting the table.

Spying him, Jamey halted in the doorway. The hand that had been tugging at the front of her shirt spread in surprise at the base of her throat. He wondered who looked guiltier.

"Is there a problem?" he asked, for lack of a better comment.

Her lips thinned as she continued into the room and opened the refrigerator. "I suppose you mean that phone conversation."

Kell rubbed the side of his neck. "I didn't mean to eavesdrop—"

"I was talking to my mother," she interrupted, a shade defiantly, rummaging in the fridge.

"In Nevada?"

"No. In Borger."

Kell bent a cockeyed tine on one fork back into place. So her mother had come with her. Jamey was probably supporting them both on the salary he'd be providing her with, and likely the reason Jamey had been concerned about living on Plum Creek, instead of in town.

She had mentioned something, or actually her mother had, about being hungry. Had Jamey been responsible for fixing her mother's meals? At the thought, a familiar tug pulled at Kell.

"You know," he said, setting plates between the silverware at each place, "it'd be a tight fit, but there's probably room for your mother in your quarters. I know Harvey had the odd relative show up now and again, and they slept on that old sofa in the alcove off the bedroom."

She turned and looked at him with that melting graygreen gaze of the first afternoon he'd met her. "That's real nice of you to offer, Kell," she said, then spied the butter on the table and reached across him to get it. Trying to get out of her path, he moved one way, she sidestepped the same, and they did an impromptu awkward dance, ending up chest to chest and eye to eye. To him, it illustrated their uneasiness with each other. The mellowness in her gaze faded, and the wariness of a few days ago returned.

"I'll keep your suggestion in mind," she said. "But Momma's taken care of in town. Besides, I'm sure your other employees have family in the area they'd like to see more of and can't. It wouldn't be fitting for me to receive special treatment."

Point taken, Kell almost said, puzzled, miffed and respecting, at once. It touched him that she was a responsible daughter, that she'd make sacrifices for her family. Yet he got the impression, as before, that Jamey was hiding something.

The room was silent as he continued setting the table, covertly observing Jamey flitting around the kitchen like a long-legged colt. And just as clumsy.

Right now she consulted a handwritten recipe on the counter. She started to measure out flour, stopped in mid-movement, and turned. "I forgot to ask—how many hands am I cookin' for?"

"Let's see." He closed one eye and squinted. "There's Charley and Purdy and Josh and Kit. And Grumpy and Dopey and Doc and Bashful," he couldn't help going on as she continued her mental tally, engagingly serious. "And don't forget the Beav."

She stared at him, banjo-eyed.

"Four," he said, with a gesture toward the set table. "Four hands, plus me. That's five," Kell calculated for her, she seemed so blamed distracted.

Jamey nodded jerkily, turning back to her work. And Kell found himself in the position of again trying to find a way to put this woman at ease.

"Coffee's good," he finally said. "Best I've tasted in a long time."

"What?" Jamey cracked an egg into the bowl, then picked pieces of shell out of it. He saw her surreptitiously check a small square of paper and tuck it back under the recipe. It dawned on him: tips from Momma.

"The coffee," he said, holding up his cup. "If this is any indication of your cooking, the boys are in for a treat."

"Uh, thanks." She gave him a brief smile, then it seemed to occur to her that the boss was making conversation with her and the polite thing would be to make it back. "Nothing like a good cup of coffee on a cold morning like this, is there?"

"Nope," Kell agreed, then frowned as a recollection struck. "I thought you said you weren't much of a coffee drinker."

She whipped back around to her work. "I'm not. Anymore. Although I might start again. Now." She took a deep breath. "My daddy always said you could take a person's measure by nothin' more than tasting the coffee they made. N-not that that's a completely reliable test."

"I see." Kell wondered at her penchant for contradicting herself. And this sagacious father of hers. What about her mother? What role had she played in her daughter's life, since clearly Jamey's father had figured greatly in her upbringing?

Then he wondered where he'd left that jar of instant and made a mental note to chuck it before the day was out.

"You seem to have been very close," he said casually. He probably shouldn't pry, but he had an interest in this father of Jamey's, now departed, and in the weight of the burden she bore that he'd glimpsed the other day, and again this morning.

"He taught me everything I know...about horses and cattle and such, that is." She pushed a lock of hair off her forehead with the back of one flour-covered hand. She didn't say what was becoming obvious to Kell, basically that no one had taught her much about cooking and, he'd bet, not a lot about cleaning, either. Not that he thought such skills fell entirely within the purview of the female sex. Left to his own devices from the time he was seven, he'd learned of necessity how to do a load of laundry and fry a hamburger patty. After years of adult bachelorhood, Kell knew his way around a kitchen.

And he knew when someone did not. Yet he had to hand it to her for doing what she'd said she would, which was try her damnedest to do the job. It was no one's fault but his own if he'd hired an incompetent cook.

But she'd needed this job, badly.

He noted the way her fingers dragged at her shirt again, and wondered at such a nervous habit. A vivid image of that straining shirtfront, up close and personal as he'd seen it a few days ago, sprang to his mind. Kell studied the dark brown coffee in his cup rather than watch her jiggling around as she mixed the contents in her bowl. So far he wasn't doing too well on his resolution not to eye her like a prize Easter ham. "Did he—your father, I mean—did he die of natural causes?" he asked.

Her movements stayed at his question. "No," she said, her face averted. "He caught meningitis. P-put him clean under in two days. Not that he was prone to sickness," she said in defense of him, as if her admission were disloyal or contradictory—again. "He'd been workin' hard, and he was run-down."

"Good God," Kell murmured, shocked by what Jamey must have endured. "And you? Your mother? Did you catch it?"

"Momma wasn't sick, but they gave her antibiotics, anyway. Daddy, too, though he was past...past..." He saw her swallow before launching into her work with renewed frenzy. She moved to the stove and turned its dials this way and that with one hand while she plucked at her shirt again with the other.

"I'm so sorry, Jamey. It must have been difficult to see him go that way."

"I don't know what it was like. I wasn't there. They wouldn't let me see him on account of I'd just found out—" Jamey set the heels of her hands on the edge of the stove, arms braced, and asked in sudden exasperation, "How in blue blazes do you turn this thing on?"

Kell could have kicked himself for being oblivious to her frustration. "Sorry. I forgot to tell you." He crossed to her side. "It's an old oven and the pilot's touchy. You've got to turn the gas on, about two hundred or so—" he demonstrated "—open the door and—see that little hole there?— blow into it once or twice. Here, you do it."

His face was side by side with hers as she puckered that lush mouth. And blew. He watched her watch the pilot catch. A faint whoosh and the oven was lit.

Jamey turned her head and almost collided noses with him. They straightened as one. "Then you adjust the, uh, temp to whatever you want," Kell instructed, feeling warm already.

"Oh." Lashes swept down as she consulted her recipe. "Four-fifty. But if I'm doubling it?" she muttered. She looked up at him again, so close. She had a smudge of flour on her nose and her full lower lip glistened rosily from being chewed on, while wisps of red hair floated around her pinkened face. She looked adorable. And about fifteen years old. He thought of her father, the loss she'd suffered. Thought about the boys, due soon, tromping in and getting a load of Jamey Dunn looking like this, soft and uncertain and utterly defenseless. They'd forget all about breakfast and start wondering what she had in the basket she was taking to Grandma's house. That's how he'd react, at least, if he were them. Which he wasn't.

He felt that protective urge again. Not to mention territorial and possessive. And just a bit predatory himself.

Her gaze registered the change in his and dropped again. "I suppose you light the griddle the same way," she said. Before he could stop her, she'd reached for the edge of the built-in metal sheet. She jerked away in pain. "Ow!"

Kell grabbed her wrist and examined the tip of her index finger and thumb, both of which were beginning to blister. "Ow is right. You'd already turned on the griddle fiddling with the dials. Come here."

He pulled her over to the sink and ran cold water over her injury, then had another look. "The best thing would be to wrap this in gauze, protect the blisters and keep them from breaking."

"But I need to finish making breakfast." She tried to pull away from him, and he started feeling warm again. "There's biscuits to bake and flapjacks to make and sausage to—heavens, the sausage!''

She broke his hold and rushed back to the stove. Lifting the lid on the skillet, she poked a fork at the links, the top half of which were gray-pink and raw, the bottom half a wizened dark brown. "I was supposed to turn them.''

"Forget the sausage,'' Kell said curtly, irritated more with himself than with her. He was letting this... this fascination with Jamey Dunn get in the way of doing his job, part of which, he realized, he'd begun to consider as taking care of her. He got the first-aid kit from the mudroom. In it he found a roll of gauze and scissors. When he motioned her over, she slanted him a look filled with that infernal wariness.

"Jamey, let me see your hand,'' he said patiently.

She extended it toward him, palm down, as if for a courtly kiss. Kell took the proffered limb and moved himself closer, managing to successfully ignore, for once, the rise in him that her touch produced. Maybe, with concentration, he could control this absorption with her.

"I take it,'' he said as he wrapped her thumb, "that when you said you didn't have much experience in the kitchen, you were actually saying you don't have any.''

She hesitated, then nodded. "I mean to do a good job though.''

"I think you will—eventually. But you're so ill-at-ease. The boys'll be in shortly, and I'm afraid that, well, with the way you're acting and the way you... look—''

"What's wrong with the way I look?'' she asked defensively.

"Nothing.'' He finished treating her hand and released it. "I mean, nothing other than....'' He decided to come right out with it. "What I'm trying to say is that you're a very pretty woman.'' When she flushed at his words, he wondered if she'd ever been told such a thing by a man before. Again it occurred to him that he'd be risking his job having this kind of employer/employee conversation in Dallas. But he simply couldn't throw her to the wolves without warning. "These men are rough and, to be frank, even if you weren't young and pretty, you'd still be the biggest distraction in a thirty-mile radius. And you just seem so easily flustered."

"I see." She stared at his chin so hard he thought he must have cut himself shaving. Or maybe it was to avoid meeting his eyes. "I can do somethin' about how I look. And as for the boys, I'll handle 'em. I know how to handle cowboys."

"I'd like to believe you, Jamey, but every time I've had a conversation with you, you've seemed pretty near ready to jump out of your skin."

Apprehension radiated from her. "What is it, Jamey?" he asked gently. "I'd like to know, would like to help if I could."

Her eyes flashed up at him then, direct and aggravated. "It's you. *You* make me nervous, chatterin' and distractin' me and hoverin' over me like a hen with a new chick."

Her vehemence surprised him. "Well, I'm glad I was here this morning or you might never've gotten the oven lit," he said in self-defense.

"It's not my fault this kitchen's got a hinky oven! And I guess I'd figure out how things worked somehow, just like everything else in this world!"

"I suppose you would," he returned. "And in the meantime I'm just expected to stand by while you struggle along, not even caring that you sear the hell out of some other body part."

"I don't *expect* you to stand by and watch me do anything! And while we're on the subject, you do that far and away too often, you know!"

"Do what?"

"Watch...me," she finished in a slightly hoarse, slightly breathy voice. And for the first time Kell realized that the attraction wasn't just on his side. And apparently just as involuntary. He couldn't suppress a swell of unadulterated masculine satisfaction.

She closed her eyes as if it was all just a little too much to handle. Then she opened them and gave him a direct view right into Jamey Dunn. "I'll admit I have some things on my mind right now. I promise I'll get over 'em or take care of 'em. But no denying I'm new to this, and I'm bound to make some...some mistakes at first." He could tell that was hard to admit. "I'd like not to make them in front of you."

Another sensation filled him—of empathy. He had the same wish of not having her see *him* screw up. He'd been irritated all morning, he realized, because he was anxious, too, about doing well, and it hadn't helped to wonder if he'd already erred in his judgment in hiring Jamey.

Yet his hunch was that he hadn't made a mistake. He did need, however, to let her find her own way. As for him— he'd have to stay on his toes. It was his responsibility to maintain control in this little preoccupation they had with each other.

"Okay," he said. "No more mother-henning in the kitchen."

She nodded.

"And I'll speak to the boys."

Her wide mouth set stubbornly. "I wish you wouldn't."

"Jamey—"

"I promise you—I'll handle it."

He paused, then shrugged his shoulders in assent. For now.

"Fine," she said. "Any other booby traps around here I should know about?"

"Not that I can think of. You do know to be careful handling raw poultry?"

She frowned. "What do you mean, handle?"

"Washing up everything in warm, soapy water when you're done cutting a chicken."

"Oh. Uh, sure."

"And you already know not to clean with ammonia and bleach at the same time, don't you? Mixing them creates a noxious gas."

She looked at him doubtfully, then her mouth turned up. "You're not makin' all this up, like those names—Dopey 'n all."

"'S'truth," he teased, then said seriously, "I'm in earnest, Jamey. I don't want to be poisoned at my dinner table or come home to a crater where my house used to be. More than that," he said softly, "I'd hate to lose... an employee."

Her gray-green eyes turned to honey again, although he sensed a firming up in the far reaches of her gaze. "Unpredictable business, this ranch stuff. Isn't it?"

"It can be. Now promise me something else. If you have questions you can't bring yourself to ask me—ask your mother."

"Yessir," she said with a dutiful air, but he got the impression that the mind wheels were turning behind those wide eyes. And that he'd started them spinning.

Kell realized they were standing there and breakfast wasn't getting any closer to made. "I'll go out and start loading hay into the pickup."

"All right," she said, continuing to regard him, fist tucked under her chin as her teeth worried the bandage on her thumb.

He lifted his hat off its peg in the mudroom and set it on his head before sliding into his heavy winter jacket. On another peg rested Jamey's beat-up, dilapidated hat. He returned to the kitchen and said, "I shouldn't have pried. About your father, that is. It's none of my business."

"That's true, it isn't," she said in that direct way of hers. "But I need to learn to deal with things. What's done is done. You know?"

Kell nodded and continued outside. The sun hadn't yet done much more than poke a lazy eyelid over the horizon.

It was quiet in the predawn, with the far-off call of a bob-white the only sound to break the silence. The light from the kitchen windows threw patchwork squares of amber on the ground. Then he heard them, coming up from the bunkhouse in a welter of jingling spurs and scuffing boots, here and there the hawk of a throat, the slap of a hat or glove against a chap-covered thigh. And all the while, a running commentary on horses and cattle and each other. Life in general for these men.

How these sounds took him back! Having a room in the main house, he'd always stood beside Bud as his uncle had greeted his men for the new day. Now Kell stood where Bud had.

Jamey wasn't the only one tackling a new challenge today. Now that the hiring was done and the meals provided for, Kell would join the hands as they made the feed runs, broke the ice on the stock tanks and repaired the windmills, whose function was so vital in winter. He knew how to perform these functions as well as any cowboy, he decided. But when the time came to make a decision of a higher order, they'd turn to him. And somehow, somewhere, he'd have to find the best answer.

Jamey had said there were a few things on her mind, that she'd get over them. Kell figured he was pretty much in the same place. He would get over them. He had to.

"Ready or not," he said to no one, "here they come."

Chapter Four

"Looks like trouble, plain and simple," was what Clan Shelton had to say about Jamey as the two men talked in Kell's office. As it so happened, Kell wouldn't accompany his men out on their rounds that morning, either. Seemed he still had a few kinks to work out in personnel, namely one Jamey Dunn.

"I don't know about that," Kell replied, leaning back in his chair and propping a boot heel on the edge of the desk.

Clan was the friend Kell had spoken of to Jamey. He lived nearby, at least in Panhandle terms; his father's spread was twenty miles away. Reid, Clan's father, ran a small but reputable cutting-horse operation. The Sheltons weren't cattlemen, but Clan had worked on Plum Creek in his teens, had learned here how to cowboy. More important, he was familiar with the ranch's workings. Clan no longer cowboyed for a living and had scaled back his involvement with his father's business a few years ago to pursue a bull-riding career. Kell was actually surprised to see him this morning, as

Clan was on the road with the rodeo nearly nonstop these days.

But he'd shown up today, and he had some advice for Kell, though not the kind Kell had anticipated when he'd made the deal with the Sheltons to let them use his cattle in training their horses in exchange for Clan's help. Part of him was inclined to tell Clan this aspect of the ranch wasn't his business; another part strove for objectivity, of which he was in short supply when it came to Jamey.

"She did a fair job this morning in an unfamiliar kitchen," he allowed.

Across the desk from him, Clan scrubbed a palm over his jaw. "I tasted those biscuits after seein' Charley gnaw off a chunk and chomp on it for two minutes. They were harder than sun-baked cow chips!"

Kell couldn't resist observing, "After chewing tobacco for twenty years, Charley's probably used to ruminating over his feed awhile. As for the flavor, I imagine his habit with snuff has pretty well numbed his taste buds, too."

He caught the sliver of a smile that touched Clan's mouth. "He didn't look to be enjoying himself," Clan said.

"He never said a word."

"He never does, but you know why he didn't today."

Kell nodded. The boys, upon seeing Jamey, had actually exhibited the personality traits of the dwarfs he'd compared them to. Charley, bandy-legged and forty, had been tongue-tied as a bashful youth. Young Josh, a slow riser, remained half asleep and unaware of the undercurrents in the kitchen. Kit, no company till he had his morning coffee, usually half a gallon of the stuff, had grumbled about the wretched edibles—as well as Josh's snoring the previous night, the way Charley ate, and everything else under creation. Then there was Purdy, legs horseshoe-bowed from decades in the saddle, oldest of the bunch and self-appointed wise man, who'd watched it all with a keen eye, his tobacco-stained handlebar mustache fairly quivering with reined amusement.

Kell watched, too, musing rather than amused, as four pairs of eyes followed Jamey's figure around the kitchen. He supposed her appearance had its advantages. The men bravely downed flapjacks the consistency of finest boot leather—Purdy's comparison, not Clan's, this time. Not that they had much choice. It was damned hard to face the bite of a wintry Panhandle morning, unthinkable on an empty stomach.

Kell had found a moment out of earshot of Jamey to apologize to the crew and guarantee things would improve. They'd seemed assured, of a fashion, but he could see them wondering what exactly was going on with their boss and his new cook. They knew that Kell was fresh to ranching; he'd made no secret of it, though he hadn't gone into detail on just what he didn't know. Maybe they were speculating on the wisdom or folly of hiring Jamey. And whether some territory had been staked out. Kell had seen Josh wake up to his surroundings, Kit get enough coffee in him to make him downright sunny, and both of the younger men wonder how to charm pretty, young Jamey. Charley and Purdy, while certainly appreciative of the view, didn't seem to have such designs. Obviously meaning to offer reassurance himself, Purdy had taken Kell aside and told him Jamey could probably serve the boys real boot leather without them noticing—as long as one item remained on the menu.

Kell had watched Jamey bestow a nervous half smile on Charley, who gazed at her with a calf-eyed look accentuated by the cud-chewing way he valiantly ate her biscuits, and had to agree, to a certain extent. *A jug of wine, a loaf of bread—and thou.* Certainly included all the major food groups *he* needed.

Yet not everyone had been so easily placated. A few minutes after the boys piled in the door, Clan Shelton had arrived and gotten a load of Jamey for the first time, as well.

"The coffee was good, at least," Kell told Clan.

"And hot. I know by the way Kit yelped when she slopped it over the edge of his mug just as I came through the door."

Kell had also noticed Jamey's reaction to Clan's appearance, as if she recognized him. As if Clan flustered her, much as Kell did. Kell wasn't eager to dwell on the ignoble emotions this thought stirred in him. Of course Jamey would have heard of Clan Shelton, a National Rodeo finalist, and would be impressed.

The secret sense of pleasure Kell had been fostering on learning of Jamey's attraction to him dwindled.

"She sure looks familiar," Clan mused.

"She's from Nevada." Then, almost having to know, he asked, "Maybe you saw her at the finals in Las Vegas last year?" He didn't like the thought of Clan picking Jamey out of a crowd, but she'd be hard to miss, with that dark red hair and long, splendid body. He knew *he'd* have noticed her.

Clan lifted his shoulders. "Could be. Hell, I've been to so many rodeos in the past year, I doubt I'd know my own face in the mirror anymore." He propped his elbows on his knees, his brow furrowed. "Anyway, that doesn't change the fact that it's obvious she doesn't have the skills to be a ranch cook. The boys might put up with the problem for a while, but these hands are used to decent grub. They'll figure they're doin' their jobs, Jamey should do hers."

"I'll admit she's green, but I think she's got the drive to make a success of this job. That's the main reason I hired her." He chewed on the inside of his cheek, wondering at Clan's continued concern with this matter. "I've learned that it's not a bad investment to take on a young, inexperienced person with a lot of enthusiasm and energy."

Clan threw Kell a sardonic look. "Yeah, but you took on one young, inexperienced—and built like a brick outhouse."

He knew his friend was joking, yet Kell found little humor in Clan's remark. "She can do the job," he said levelly, realizing he echoed Jamey's own words to him. And perhaps sounded as stubborn and ignorant of what she was taking on.

Clan sat back and sighed. "Well, it's your operation. I'm just thinkin' you've got one ambitious schedule set to bring this place around, and while I think you can do it, you don't have much room to make mistakes."

"I realize that, but I don't see how hiring Jamey as a cook and housekeeper will have that much negative impact."

"Why take a chance?"

Kell dug his thumbnail into a gouge in the scarred desktop and said nothing for a moment. Wasn't that the same question he'd asked himself since Jamey had walked into his life? Yet he knew why. Though Kell had yet to resolve his doubts about his intuition regarding the land, the horses and his cattle, he believed in his ability to judge people. He wasn't willing to discount the gut feeling that had led him to take Jamey on—because he believed the same impulse had led him to taking on Plum Creek. He'd felt very strongly her accord on his mission. She'd said she wanted to help him achieve his goal, though he didn't see her doing it as a ranch hand, not even as a cook, but as a . . . an ally.

It occurred to Kell that this was slightly different thinking from even a few days ago. Then, he'd hired Jamey because it was what Bud would have done; because, Kell had thought at the time, he'd wanted in a sense to fill Bud's role of providing sanctuary for someone in need, as Kell himself had been taken in. Now, though, he knew it was *his* need of Jamey to fill a role in his life that influenced him. And yet this decision, too, had little to do with prudent business judgment, but more with that sense of wanting to become closer to the values that were most important in life.

"Look, Clan," Kell finally said. "Having to train a new cook is not going to cause much of a setback. The position isn't as vital as a ranch hand spot. Besides, where would I find someone else at this point to live in?"

"That's true," Clan admitted.

"And I can't afford to spend much more time here, taking care of meals and interviewing. I need to be out with the men, helping them and getting a firsthand look at things so I can make informed decisions on matters when they do come up."

Again, Clan scraped his hand up the side of his face and through his black hair. "I guess it won't cost much to give it a shot. And, like I said, it's your ranch. I was just thinkin' that there's bound to be unexpected setbacks croppin' up along the way. Why allow a possible problem into the picture?"

Kell looked his friend in the eye. "Let's just say I'm willing to take the risk."

Rising, Clan hesitated as he scrutinized Kell. "It's none of my business, either, but I'd hate to see you get foolish about a woman and let it hinder your prospects."

"What do you mean?"

Clan's green eyes were speculative as he stared out the window. "Only that the things you've wanted for yourself for years can change like that when a woman enters into the equation."

"I see." Kell recalled that Reid Shelton had told him how Clan had postponed his rodeo career in order to stay on their ranch while Clan's mother suffered through a lengthy illness before dying a few years ago. And, Kell also remembered, that a woman had come to train her cutting horse under Reid's tutelage . . . a young, inexperienced and pretty woman, from Reid's account. Suddenly his friend's attitude, his objections to Jamey, fell into place. Clan seemed driven in a way that had nothing to do with the competitions he rode in. Kell wondered if a man needed that drive to succeed in this environment, wondered if he had it, or if he'd find out only at such time when he'd have to call upon some reaction that had no root in rational thought. He recalled the arm-wrestling match with Jamey that ended up having nothing to do with strength or even proving a point. Kell wasn't positive he wanted those traits to be part of what motivated him.

Regardless, he looked at his friend's conflicted features and made a mental note to access Clan's time only in instances of true importance. He gave Clan a sympathetic smile. "I'll be sure to keep my wits about me," he promised.

"Ain't your wits that's doin' the thinkin' in situations like this," his friend drawled, the joking nature of the comment belied by its rueful inflection.

After Clan left, Kell made his way to the kitchen and found it empty, though clean. No sight of Jamey, yet it was hours to lunchtime. He wondered what she'd attempt for that meal. Well, he'd agreed to leave her to her own devices.

He should check on Josh and Kit's progress in cleaning out the barns and help them prioritize the outbuildings to patch first, as nearly all of them had fallen into some state of disrepair. Charley and Purdy were making feed runs right now and continuing to inspect the pregnant heifers and pin down an estimate of calves they could expect to be born this spring. Charley had mentioned at breakfast that in the north pasture there was a dry creek bed, steep in places, that a few cows favored. He wanted to know if Kell thought it best to build new fence around the area or just keep checking it regularly till spring, when they'd be able to tell if it might fill up enough to be a fair water source.

The only way to find out was to have a look. It'd probably be a judgment call. And he had to make his mistakes and get some experience under his belt, just like Jamey.

Jamey put more elbow grease into scouring the pot in the sink. After half an hour of hard work, she'd barely made a dent in the gunk covering the bottom. She sniffed the air with relief. At least the scorched food odor had tapered off.

Which was what Kell observed a minute later when he walked into the kitchen and poured himself a cup of coffee.

"I closed the window only a few minutes ago," she confessed, stifling a wince at plunging her hands into soapy dishwater to hide them from Kell. After a week at Plum Creek, she had a few more battle scars to go with the burnt fingertips of her first morning: scraped knuckles acquired when grating potatoes for hash browns, a cut along the side of one finger where she'd nicked it slicing okra. The water stung like all get-out, but she didn't want Kell seeing her wounds and thinking her prone to accidents, or that he needed to doctor her every little owie.

"The odor was a little overwhelming," Kell said diplomatically. "You're getting better, though."

"'Getting better at stinkin' the whole place up to be damned' was how Purdy put it," she said with brutal honesty.

Kell leaned back against the edge of the counter and chuckled. "Well, so this meal wasn't a particular success. I do think you've made progress with breakfast."

She wasn't going to point out that, one, it would have been hard to get much worse and, two, she darn well better be getting the hang of it. After all, she'd fixed the same thing day in and day out for the past week. She knew the boys were getting weary of the same fare, but Glenna had refused to let Jamey move on to corned-beef hash or even grits until she got reasonably proficient at a few dishes. The hands, for the most part, held their tongues; Jamey figured because they weren't sure what the trade-off might be in a more diverse selection.

Kell, also, had said nothing, though a lot went on behind that chestnut gaze of his. He'd kept his promise to let her make her own mistakes, though she noticed he still seemed to watch out for her. His concern touched her, and she had to guard against the inclination to tell him her story, to get his help in figuring out how to resolve complications that were no one's fault or responsibility but her own.

At least she'd been able to resolve one problem. She'd driven into town and made a minor raid on a discount Western-wear store. She'd gotten some relaxed-fit jeans and made sure they relaxed a lot in the seat and thighs. Then she'd bought a couple of extra-large men's shirts. Jamey glanced down at herself. She defied anyone to find her attractive in shapeless duds like these. She knew she'd gotten the right effect when the hands had trooped in and she'd seen the light go clean out of their weather-beaten faces. Oh, they still saw her as a woman, but not one up for grabs, so to speak.

So her plan had worked—except on Kell. He was careful, but she caught the private inspection he gave her when he thought she or the hands wouldn't notice. It was that smoldering look. And it confounded her. How could a man find a woman dressed like a cornfield scarecrow appealing? It didn't make sense.

She ventured a glance at Kell as he sipped his coffee, one heel propped upon the booted instep of his other foot as he watched her. Jamey directed her attention back to the pot in her hand and tried to ignore the tingles of sensation that swept over her like a sand-laden gust of wind on a hot day. Maybe it wasn't the way a cowboy's mind worked that eluded her, just as it probably wasn't her *mind* that made her skin pop out in gooseflesh.

She had to stop thinking, or feeling, or whatever she was doing that made her find Kell Hamilton as fascinating as a double rainbow in a mother-of-pearl sky.

It struck her that this was the perfect time to put her plan into effect.

"So, um, did you decide what to do with that washout Charley talked about?" she asked conversationally.

From behind her, she heard Kell shift his feet. "Yes."

When he said nothing more, she prompted him. "Are you going to fence it?"

"No, not yet. I'm guessing Bud would have fenced it off before if it was a real problem. It's dry now, but it might be a draw, with water close to the surface. I've decided to let it alone for now. This spring, we'll see whether it fills up and how much. With little live water on the place, it'd be foolish to discount a source without checking it out thoroughly."

"If it gets real spongy, though, you might lose a cow or calf to coyotes or a cougar trapping it down there. And I don't think you want them coming around, thinking the washout is a choice spot for an easy meal."

Out of the corner of her eye she saw Kell, a frown on his face, set his coffee cup down. She let him mull over that information while she drained the dishwater from the sink. Jamey gave the scorched pan a baleful look and wondered if it was ruined. Later tonight she'd give her mother a call and ask. And talk to Hettie, which she just had to do, silly as it seemed. Jamey was terrified the baby would forget her and so was prepared to go to great lengths to prevent that from happening. Thoughts of her child hovered in the back of her mind constantly, causing her heart to ache just a little all the time. But she'd exhausted the options that would keep them together. And this setup *was* temporary.

Drying her hands on a towel, she turned to face Kell. For once he was staring at something other than her as he seemed caught up in his thoughts. She experienced a surge of satisfaction, believing it had been her comment that got him thinking.

"Of course," she went on with studied casualness, "in my experience, Brangus are generally a manageable breed. You could probably keep 'em steered clear of that area without much effort. I'm surprised any of them got that rangy."

"It's this Brahman who's got a fondness for the place."

"Oh. Well, that explains it. Brahmans can be bull-headed." She smiled at her unintentional joke.

He looked at her then—and smiled, too. It was a glorious sight. His face was shaped by clean, strong angles that would have seemed severe on a man with less stature. She noticed how he filled the room with his height. But then, she was used to her father doing that, though Kell didn't carry the weight her father had. His body was more sinewy. Henry, on the other hand, had the size and build of a rodeo cowboy, small and compact.

And she had better things to do than to stand there and mentally compare one man to another.

"I wonder why Bud kept her around?" Kell pondered out loud.

"Oh, it's a cow?" Jamey asked. "For some reason I'd been thinking it was a bull." Again striving for offhandedness, she rested her weight on one hip and sank her hands into her back pockets. "Your uncle probably kept her because she was a sturdy and reliable calver. And fierce enough to protect her baby from predators."

"Could be. She certainly is big. And bullheaded, like you said. Kicked me in the shin when Charley and I finally got a loop over her head to drag her out of there."

"Are you hurt?" Jamey asked in alarm.

"Just a bruise." He shrugged off her concern. He took in her expression, then the rest of her, head to toe, bringing back the tingly feeling.

This time she decided to confront him, because he had to stop looking her over like a T-bone steak he couldn't decide which end to cut into first. "What are you starin' at?" she asked bluntly, straightening her shoulders and throwing out her chin in challenge.

For a moment he continued to scrutinize her, puzzled, then shook his head as if clearing it. "Sorry. I was thinking of something Purdy said. About, uh, menus." He, too, slid his weight onto one hip as he braced the heel of one hand on the edge of the counter behind him. Still regarding her intently, he said with almost reluctant emphasis, "I don't know why, but I get the feeling this cow won't be worth the problems she might cause me."

She'd been pondering his comment about menus, and so nearly missed the one that made her question whether she and Kell were talking about cattle—or something else.

Jamey yanked her fingers out of her pockets and pivoted away from him, finding credible motivation in readying the kitchen for tomorrow's adventures in cooking. Her back to him, she gave in to the need to temporarily relieve the pressure on her breasts, now hidden by the loose shirt, by pulling at the elastic that bound them. Her mother had told her this was the best way to eventually stop her milk, in addition to hot baths. But after a week, the discomfort had eased little, and Jamey wondered how much longer she'd have to endure feeling like she carried around two filled-to-bursting water balloons on her chest. Not having to be jostled around on horseback at this particular time was probably a fortunate development, because it looked like it'd be a while till she stopped lactating if the mere mention of motherhood—human or bovine—brought her milk in.

And a ways to go to feeling comfortable with her plan. Ridiculous of her to think Kell had been issuing some veiled concern in hiring her. He hadn't been talking about *her* being stubborn or worth the problems she might cause for sturdy offspring...and he couldn't *begin* to suspect about Hettie. Jamey made herself take a deep breath. Yes, ridiculous. It was her own conscience that pricked at her for concealing her motherhood, for maneuvering him with her not-so-idle advice.

She wasn't deceiving him. She *did* know ranching and cows.

Jamey began sorting out silverware. "Any extra men tomorrow?" she asked, hoping to put the last subject behind them, almost out of temptation's reach. Deception was not her strong suit. Yet her question had its circuitous purpose, as well. Reid Shelton had stopped by late afternoon and had stayed to supper—much to his regret, she guessed, though Reid, a mid-fortyish, fine-looking man, had been a perfect gentleman.

"No," Kell answered. "We'll rarely have either of the Sheltons as guests."

"Especially now that they know I'm far from challenging anyone in a chuckwagon cook-off," Jamey predicted, again trying to be honest—almost in an effort to make up for being not quite so honest with Kell a second ago. Nor now.

There was a pause before Kell said quietly, "Don't be so hard on yourself, Jamey." Though he stood close by, she sensed rather than actually saw the hand he held out toward her, then dropped as if remembering himself. He wanted to offer support, seemed almost second nature for him to do so.

But she didn't *want* him to comfort her, to understand her. Why couldn't he be more of a cowboy, self-absorbed, or like her father, who never made excuses for anyone?

"Yessir," Jamey answered Kell, falling back on the more formal address to keep him at a distance.

He sighed. Tuned to a country-western station, the radio on the counter filled the room with tinny music. She had gotten in the habit of turning it on as she cleaned up from supper, and it didn't strike Jamey as particularly amusing to hear Willie Nelson admonishing mothers not to let their babies grow up to be cowboys. Ol' Willie had the right of it. In fact, she'd go him one better and recommend that mothers not let their babies marry cowboys or otherwise associate with them, either.

"I hope, at least," she said, filling the gap in conversation, "that I've taken care of...you know, the situation with the boys. And me."

He shot her a quizzical glance.

Her cheeks heated up. "My new clothes."

"Oh." Kell smiled again, a hint of the devil in his eyes, making him look roguish in a way Henry could only dream of.

She had a lamentable penchant for discovering new ways to fall for this cowboy.

"You'll do," he said. Then his smile died and he peered at her, suddenly intense. "Speaking of the Sheltons, had you met Clan before the other day?"

She nearly dropped a stack of plates. So she *was* going to find out the answer to her question. Jamey had been walking on eggs since Clan Shelton had shown up, wondering if he recognized her. With Clan riding the rodeo, she knew he'd seen her with Henry. She couldn't help thinking it was a matter of time before Clan connected her back to her ex-husband.

"I don't know Clan personally," she answered Kell's question with care. "Anyone who's followed the rodeo would've heard of him, though."

"And you follow the rodeo?"

"No. I mean, I've been to my share of 'em. I understand it's not much of a life." That was an understatement. And hitting a little too close. Though she saw her failed marriage as just that, a failure, she was willing to own up to it. However, if Clan knew she was Henry's ex, and he met up with Henry somewhere down the road.... Jamey wasn't prepared to have Henry know her whereabouts right now. Not that he'd go out of his way and come looking for her. No, she'd have to fall into his lap like the first time. But say he did—she'd have to tell him about Hettie. And she couldn't, not yet. She was determined, however, to be as honest as possible with Kell.

"I've seen Clan ride. He always seems to be one of the cowboys who'd make an impression on a woman." *Definitely* too close. "I never actually met him till the other morning.'' She decided to go at it head-on. "Why? Did he say he knew me?''

"Not...exactly.'' At his hesitation, her gaze flew to his as she panicked. Perhaps he knew about her and Henry already, and this whole pretense of hiding Hettie could end, and she'd take her chances forthrightly with Kell.

Yet she found no accusation or suspicion in his brown eyes, though they were even more intense. "Clan thought you might have looked familiar, but it was probably because, like you said, you'd run in the same circles.''

"Oh.'' Another reason for Kell's questions occurred to her. "I hope you don't think I'm one of those belt buckle bunnies who's easy to impress with a rodeo win, a smile, or a smooth line,'' she said with utter conviction and an obvious message of caution—for them both. She wasn't a woman to repeat her mistakes. "No, sir. Not me.''

She could tell she surprised him with her vehemence, but instead of putting the fear of God in him, Kell Hamilton suddenly grinned, almost in relief. "I'm glad to hear it.''

"You are?''

"Yes, ma'am,'' he answered with a drawl, mimicking her formal address, though he sounded in no way proper. He sounded sexy and seductive as ever a cowboy could.

Jamey had never been more confused. At times he seemed not at all like the kind of man she'd learned to be wary of, making her feel an urge to unburden herself to him. *This* man just might understand...then he went and got all cowboy on her! Jamey decided she was out of her everloving mind, which led her to conclude it would be best to keep quiet. Yet she needed to pursue her goal to prove to Kell she could handle the job.

Which job? The question popped into her head.

On reflex, she crossed her arms over her breasts, almost to shield from examination those she held in her heart—her father, her mother, Hettie—and how she perceived them. Or they perceived her.

At her movement, Kell's eyes drifted downward, alighting on a point of interest, for he reached out—and this time his hand completed its course and closed over hers.

"What happened here?" he asked, touching her scraped knuckle, then the cut.

"Hazards of the trade," Jamey said pointedly. "You know, like your kick in the shin?"

"Mmm," he said, noncommittal. She studied his downturned features. He looked tired and worried, and it disturbed her that she hadn't noticed that before.

Her gaze wandered to his jawline, where he had a dark, flat mole—a large freckle really—just on the underside of his jaw, midway between chin and earlobe. She'd noticed it that first morning when she'd stood this close to him. On a woman, she'd have called it a beauty mark, yet there was nothing feminine about it. His smile, his eyes, she could understand, but she had no idea why this mole mesmerized her. Maybe it was because, like her own freckles, they undoubtedly resided on other places on his body. And she was dying to know where, how many, and in what pattern.

She wanted to move away, out of the circle of warmth emanating from his body, out of the range of his influence. But she needed to learn how to stand up to this man. So she held her ground, though in actuality it was Kell who held her, captivated her as he'd done the other day. He even took her other hand in his opposite one, his fingers lightly grasping hers as his thumbs slid bumpily across her knuckles. She tried not to squirm.

"I'll admit," he murmured, "that I'm finding it quite a hazardous experience dealing with ill-tempered cows like that blasted Brahman. And it's not just my own hide I'm thinking about. Josh was on the ground checking a fence post today when a bull—that a minute before had been eating hay, perfectly content—turned on him and charged. Tried to get into his back pocket, as Purdy said. Josh had to scramble like mad over that fence, barely escaping getting pitched, while the rest of them sat on the tail of the pickup, laughing fit to be tied."

Jamey couldn't prevent a small snort of scorn. "Well, first thing is, no bull is ever 'perfectly content.' And you never turn your back on one. If the boys were laughing, that's why. Would've served Josh right if he got stomped." Then, because she wanted both to demonstrate her knowledge as well as to distance herself emotionally from this man, if she couldn't put physical distance between them, Jamey added bluntly, "Served you right, getting kicked by the Brahman. If you knew anything about the breed, they can't be trusted farther than you can throw 'em."

"Really?" Kell said, finally dropping her hands. "*You* seem to know an awful lot about cattle."

She was glad he'd stopped touching her, but she wasn't thrilled with the sudden change in his tone. "I told you I did. I grew up on a ranch."

"And you seem quite willing to share your wisdom with me."

Jamey resisted the urge to fidget under his examination. "I just want to . . . to help you."

"That's certainly what you said when you took the job here." His mouth tightened. "I can see what you're doing, Jamey."

"What's that?"

"Trying to show me what you know about cowboying so I'll give you a job at it."

Jamey had the grace to blush. So much for her being any good at deception. "Well, and what if I am?" she demanded, going on the offensive. "I do know a lot, and it seems like you could really use my advice."

Slowly, Kell brought himself upright. "Could I now?"

"Sure you could," she asserted, even as she got the impression she was painting herself into a corner. "You should take advantage of me. My *experience*." She felt her face turn even pinker. No wonder he eyed her all the time when she ran up such bright red flags.

He didn't seem to register her slip of the tongue. "You might very likely know what you're talking about with ranching," he said. "But I still can't believe you know what you'd be getting into as a ranch hand."

"Because I'm a woman!"

"No, because—" He broke off with a shake of his head, and she wondered what he'd been about to say. Palm pressed to the countertop and arm locked at the elbow as he leaned upon it, his other hand propped on his hip, Kell looked like a man out of patience, discouraged. Or disappointed. In her. The thought that he might be caused a sting behind Jamey's eyes. She started getting that desperate feeling again that had plagued her for months now. Yet again, her prospects were waning. She needed this job!

She searched for an argument. "Why couldn't I know what I'm talkin' about? You seem to know about cooking and cleaning."

"I do know *something* about them, but you'll notice I'm not holding myself out as a professional housewife!"

They stood toe-to-toe, chests nearly touching. Deep brown eyes stared down into hers. As she'd observed before, there were few men Jamey had to look up to, and she didn't like one bit that Kell Hamilton had that advantage over her. It wasn't that great a distinction, but every detail made a difference right now in his forming an opinion about her.

Because he had to stop seeing her as a woman. She didn't want his protection. Didn't need it. But she did want him to be a different kind of cowboy. Otherwise she had little chance of convincing him *she* could be one.

Jamey set her jaw so hard she was sure she'd crack a molar in the next minute. "I can do the job. I've done it before."

Kell's jaw bulged, as well. "You've got a job to do already, and I've yet to see you do it well."

She blinked. "That," she stated, "was cold."

The lift of his brow seemed to say she couldn't have it both ways. "You want to prove yourself, Jamey?" he asked. "You want to help me? You've already got the opportunity."

Fine. If that's how he wanted it, that's how he'd get it. No more hand-holding or significant looks or chummy little pacts just between the two of them in the predawn hours.

Tempted to give him a boot in his other shin, she said, her throaty voice pitched at its most masculine, "Yessir."

Kell's mouth twisted as he marked her formal address. Then his eyes darkened, pupils dilating as they had the other day in the middle of their arm wrestle.

Did it again, didn't you, girl? Jamey thought just as he said, "Oh, one more thing."

Abruptly he slipped an arm around her waist and pulled her to him. Cradling her nape in his other hand, he dipped his head, and his mouth found hers, swiftly and surely. She should have seen it coming, but she hadn't—not until the split second beforehand—and so she was too startled to pull away, to shove him back, to even breathe, as his lips, firm and determined, molded to hers in a fiery kiss. Before she'd barely had time to register the feel of him holding her, he let her go.

He looked her up and down—again!—with a wry lift of both eyebrows. "Just checking. For a minute there, you had me wondering what you were really hiding under those clothes." He smiled rakishly. "And whether I should take advantage of you." Touching the tip of his index finger to his temple in a salute, he said, "G'night, *ma'am.*"

With that, he strode out of the kitchen, leaving her blushing and sputtering—and hotter than a match head.

When Jamey finally found her voice, she flung the most scathing insult that came to mind at his long-departed back.

"Good night—*cowboy*."

Chapter Five

"**Y**ou," Glenna observed, causing Jamey to glance up at her, "are shameful."

"That I am," Jamey conceded with an unrepentant grin. It was her day off, the third since she'd started at Plum Creek, and the three of them—Jamey, Glenna and Hettie—were in their Sunday finest, having gone to church that morning. They were now sitting in a booth at a local café, enjoying dinner. And precious time together.

Jamey turned back to the occupation that had earned her mother's admonishment, that of talking outrageous baby talk to her daughter, who lay in her portable car seat next to Jamey.

"*You* not shameful," she crooned to the child. "You was just the best girl in church this mornin', not like those other young whelps who yipped and whined and had to be taken out." She poked a gentle finger into Hettie's tummy and gave it a wiggle. "That's 'cause you's a big girl, four months old, and the smartest baby in the *whole* country. Isn't that right?"

Hettie kicked her booted feet and waved her arms in agreement. Round, brown eyes turned into crescents of pleasure as the baby grinned, exposing shiny pink gums, before she crammed her fist into her mouth and gooed around it. She was especially cute in a new red corduroy jumper and gingham blouse that Glenna had sewn for her. Warm, white tights completed the ensemble, and Jamey thought that even a perfect stranger would find her daughter irresistible today. She knew she did.

Having downed her food, she pushed her plate away and lifted Hettie under the armpits to sit on the edge of the table facing her. The little head lolled as the baby turned her face this way and that, curious about her surroundings.

"She'll drool on your new outfit," Glenna warned moderately.

"And hers," Jamey said, which was more her concern, though she did appreciate Glenna's sewing efforts in the form of the sage-colored dress of jersey wool Jamey wore. She reached for a cloth and daubed Hettie's lower lip, catching a dribble before it fell. Hettie stuck out her tongue at the contact, and the two of them played sample the washcloth. Then Hettie seemed to realize that while the texture was curious enough, taste and satisfaction left something to be desired. She gave a kick and a whine.

"*Still* hungry? Or just restless?" Jamey asked. Holding on to the baby with one hand, she reached in the diaper bag for a fresh bottle of formula. "Is this what you want, sugar bump?" She teased the nipple over Hettie's upper gum before pulling back to peer into the round face in front of her.

Hettie blinked. Then her eyes crinkled as she let out a howl.

Hurriedly, Jamey tucked the baby against her midriff and popped the nipple into her mouth. With little puckers in her forehead where eyebrows had yet to appear, Hettie stared up at her mother and went to town on the bottle like she hadn't eaten in a month. Shaking her head, Jamey looked up at her own mother, who raised her well-defined brows.

"Don't get in the way of that girl and her dinner," she told Jamey even as she gave her granddaughter a fond glance. "You were the same way at that age." She nodded toward the burp cloth on the table. "You might want to protect your dress with that."

"Yes'm," Jamey mumbled, complying. She thought to add, "Thanks again for makin' it for me. It fits perfect." The dress's skirt was long, hitting Jamey's legs mid-calf and swirling around them. The neckline was high but fitted, as were the sleeves and bodice, which tapered to a drop waist. Though it was a simply designed dress, Jamey felt as awkward as a three-legged calf, completely out of place. Her mother had persuaded her to wear her hair unbraided and caught back from her face with two large barrettes, and it swung around her face unfamiliarly. She pushed it back over her shoulder when Hettie's saliva-coated fist began a wobbly course toward it.

Glenna gave her handiwork a critical eye. "I was afraid the dress'd be tight across the bust, but I didn't want to make it too big, since I knew you'd be losing inches there as soon as you stopped nursing."

"Well, you guessed just right." Jamey ran an absent hand over the soft material across her collarbone, resisting the urge to pluck at it. She'd stopped producing milk a few weeks ago and had gone down a cup size in her bras, which she no longer filled to overflowing. She supposed she'd also lost a little weight from sheer hard work. And worry.

Her chin dropped as her gaze roamed over her daughter's face, one velvet cheek tucked against her breast, well protected by layers of wool and quilted cloth, and she missed with all her heart the connection that had made her feel truly a mother.

The only thing that saved her from despair was knowing she could fascinate and delight Hettie with the mere sound of her husky voice. She could sing lullabies in that voice, with its cracks and croaks, and soothe her daughter's cries, her fears, to nothing but soft sighs. It made Jamey hope that somehow, some way, despite the separation, she'd managed to maintain a connection with her baby that was theirs alone.

The baby's mouth worked with that automatic rhythm, her gaze shifting as a bit of color or noise caught her attention. Jamey lifted one tiny hand to her lips and blew a raspberry on its dimpled knuckles, bringing Hettie's attention back to her. Button eyes widened, fascinated, and the suction pump ground to a momentary halt before it started up again with renewed vigor.

Jamey thought her heart would turn over and expire with loving this child.

Tenderly she arranged the ruffles on her baby's blouse. "Thanks, too, Momma, for Hettie's dress. And all the other things you do for us."

"It's my pleasure. Keeps me busy. She's a good baby, doesn't take much of my time."

"I—I think she knows me, don't you?" Jamey mused, still staring into her daughter's face and shaking her chubby, creased wrist gently. "Even though I'm not around?"

"Of course she does, sugar."

No, Jamey didn't picture herself sewing her daughter perky little outfits, and maybe she didn't know every in and out of the baby's feeding schedule, but she *was* mother to this child, seeing to her welfare—even if it took her away from Hettie.

"Jamey, I can see you doing it again," Glenna said.

Jamey lifted her head. "Doing what?"

"You come home every Saturday evening nearly skippin' with joy—and then it's all downhill from there. You start thinkin' about how things are and you get this faraway, pining look on your face, and by the time you leave Sunday night you're lower than a river bottom." She paused in cutting into her chicken-fried steak. "Are you doing any better with your duties?"

"Oh, yes. The housework is under control and doesn't take as much time since I got that first cleaning out of the way. For a while it seemed every surface or whatnot I laid eyes on needed to be dusted, washed or polished. The place fairly shines now," Jamey boasted.

"And your cookin'?"

"It's comin' along." She set the bottle on the table and shifted the baby to her shoulder, one palm anchoring Hettie's padded bottom, the other patting her back. "I'm down to about one flop a week."

"Any closer to gettin' a chance at being a hand?"

"No," Jamey said with a bitter tinge.

"Then it seems to me you might want to keep the cooking and housekeeping job and forget about the ranch hand position."

Jamey stared at her mother as if she'd grown horns. "But that's what I do best! I'm no cook—not permanently, at least."

She realized why Glenna might have suggested she keep the housekeeping job. "Of course, if I was out riding cattle all day, I still wouldn't be able to care for Hettie. If I was cookin' and cleanin' around the ranch house, I'd be able to see to her myself and be a real mother to her," she said, finishing with the self-censure that inevitably shaded her opinion of herself these days. "Is that what you think I should do, Momma?" she asked achingly. "Give up on cowboying and concentrate on mothering?"

"I was thinking of you, sugar. You're tearin' yourself up inside, it seems, trying to fill both pairs of boots."

Jamey had to admit the option was darned tempting. "I guess there're worse livings," she murmured, absently rubbing Hettie's spine. "I just always thought of myself as a cowgirl. It's what I know how to do." And what would get her back to a normal life. "It's who I am, like Daddy was a cowboy."

"But you never thought of yourself as a mother before you had Hettie, and you're doin' a fine job at that."

Jamey met her mother's eyes and tried not to get choked up. Her emotions on that subject were too volatile to debate. Yet perhaps the time had arrived for some of the words they'd been avoiding to be uttered.

"I sure made a mess of being a wife, didn't I?" Never before had she made such an admission. Now that she had, she made herself go on. "And pickin' a husband."

Glenna's gray eyes softened. "That was an unfortunate mistake, Jamey, but it doesn't mean you couldn't be a good wife to some deserving man."

Jamey fixed her gaze on the crust of Texas toast left on her plate. And swallowed as a lump rose in her throat. She refused to bawl like a baby right here in broad daylight surrounded by strangers. Maybe now wasn't the time to discuss this. But her heart was so full. So confused. "Oh, Momma."

Glenna set down her knife and fork. "What, sugar?"

"M-maybe I was never meant to be a wife in the first place."

"Why would you think that?"

"A wife should stand by her husband, like you always did Daddy. You supported him in everything he did. I—I think a man needs to know a woman will do that for him."

"That was my way of dealing with things, certainly. It doesn't mean it's the only way two people can share their life together." Glenna cleared her throat as if a lump resided there, as well. "Marriage isn't like a dance, with the man leading and the woman following along best she can." There was a hint of rebuke in her voice that Jamey picked up on.

"You mean, it takes two to tango," she said with a gesture toward the child against her shoulder. "Right?"

"One partner should never carry all the blame—or the burden," Glenna said emphatically, then went on more gently. "Not just you, and not just Henry. But it's no sin you divorced him. He wasn't interested in workin' on the marriage. It's to your credit it didn't take you but a few months to figure that out."

"How do I know that, though?" Jamey asked, voicing the doubt she'd lived with for a year. "How do I know that with love and understanding, he might not've turned into a decent husband?"

"I guess you'll never know—because he never gave *you* the chance."

Jamey lowered Hettie into the crook of her arm and offered the bottle to the baby, who roused herself from half sleep to have another go at it. Jamey rocked her daughter. Her daughter—and Henry's. She knew she must find him soon. Even if he hadn't been a very good husband, he might be a good father. He deserved that chance, at the very least.

"I don't hate him, y'know," she confided. "I don't think I could. It either isn't in me, or it isn't in him to be hated. Henry wasn't a bad man. He was just a . . . a cowboy."

"So, is Kell Hamilton just a cowboy, too?"

Jamey's chin shot up. "What?"

Glenna shrugged. "I mean, you said at first he was like your father, but if you're no closer to convincing him you can be a good hand, does that mean he's like the other ranchers you approached before comin' to Texas?"

"Oh." For a second Jamey had been afraid her mother had discerned the attraction between her and Kell that had grown even stronger in the past weeks despite the rift between them. What *was* it about her and cowboys? "I don't know if I'll get a chance at the job or not. Kell is just about dead set against it. But then sometimes, he seems different. He's real . . . encouraging of me. He doesn't stint on praise, but it doesn't seem forced, either." Jamey wondered if she blushed. Thinking about Kell and the instances he'd acted that way certainly produced a glow in her. "But other times—" she broke off, then went on with an impatient huff, "He *insists* on seein' me as a woman."

Glenna laughed before saying on a regretful sigh, "Oh, Jamey. You *are* a woman."

"Well, he balks like a mule when I give him advice. If it were Purdy or Charley that was offerin' an opinion, you can be sure he'd listen. But they don't seem to tell him what to do."

"Mmm. So tell me, what would *you* do if Kell made you a ranch hand on Plum Creek?" She stayed Jamey's response with an upheld hand. "Not what you'd do then, but later. I mean, what do you see this job doing for yours and Hettie's future?"

"It'll give me the chance to build a reputation for myself, enough so I'd be able to be a ranch manager on a spread someday. It wouldn't have to be a big place. I'm not lookin' for that kind of responsibility. Just so long as the owner had the confidence in me to let me run the operation as I saw fit."

"And then what do you see?"

Jamey closed her eyes, quite willing to feature this next scene, she'd done it so often before. "I see a redheaded girl jumping off the school bus and racin' into the house to change so she can get on her horse and find her... find me, and be my little helper. My righthand man."

The image was so vivid, she started to get choked up again, even more so when she heard Glenna's gentle admonishment. "You can't rewrite the past, sugar."

Jamey opened her eyes. "I'm not tryin' to, Momma. But is it wrong to want to raise my daughter the way I was?"

Now Glenna closed her eyes. "I don't know. I just hate having you think you've got to do it all. Or do it all alone." Her lids fluttered open with the slight shake of her head, as if to escape visions of her own. "Well, so back to gettin' you that ranch hand position. What do you plan to do?"

Jamey nibbled her lower lip. "I've been thinkin' about that. There's this little mare I've seen in the corral. None of the boys ever take her out, so I'd bet she's too unpredictable for them, or she hasn't been trained to handle stock. I thought if I couldn't get Kell to give me a shot out on the range for real, maybe I could work with the mare and show him what I could do with her on the few cows they've got penned."

"That might work." Glenna toyed with a string bean on her plate. "Or you might try a different tack with Kell."

"Such as?"

"Don't be so mannish, be more... feminine."

"But I'm trying *not* to be." Had her mother heard nothing she'd said? "It's not goin' to get me anywhere. I mean, you should see the look in his eyes when—" She bit her tongue. "I told you, I'm not like that," she went on. "I'm not like you, supportive and agreeable—"

"I don't *want* you to be like me!" Glenna interrupted, the fierceness of her statement surprising Jamey. Then she gave an impatient huff the carbon copy of her daughter's earlier one. "I'm just sayin' it's not the real you that he's gettin' to know. Would it be so terrible to have Kell see you certainly as a competent hand with your own opinions and views about things, but also as someone who might add a little more to what he's trying to accomplish—*because* you're a woman and a mother?"

"You aren't suggestin' that I *try* to get Kell Hamilton interested in me that way?"

"No... well, maybe. You just said he was different from Henry. Encouraging and accepting and dependable."

"And that's a fine reason to admire a man—isn't it?— because he seems likely to stick around." Jamey realized she was drawing stares. She leaned forward and whispered loudly, "I'm not interested in *him!*"

"But there's a spark between you, isn't there?"

So Glenna had noticed! Jamey's face flamed. "I was clean gone on Henry, too, and look where that got me. I can't believe you're even suggestin' I get involved with a cowboy again!"

"Jamey, you can't hold up your experience with Henry as the only way it can be with a man, just as it didn't work to hold up the image you had of your daddy and expect Henry to fit into it."

Jamey stared at a stain on the wallpaper behind the salt and pepper shakers. She got the feeling this was one of those subjects she'd been avoiding so hard. And the one she most wanted to continue avoiding.

Out of the corner of her eye, she saw Glenna's shoulders slump in discouragement. She, too, looked nice today in the homemade turquoise dress that brought out the pink in her complexion. Her mother had half her life ahead of her—and she probably didn't want to spend the rest of it seeing to her grandchild, while Jamey got her own life together. *That*, Jamey concluded, was the reason for this conversation about keeping the cook job and letting Kell get to know her. If she and Hettie were installed, in whatever capacity, at Plum Creek, Glenna would be relieved of her obligations toward her daughter and granddaughter.

Was that such a terrible prospect? She thought of Kell, of how he saw her, and Jamey knew it wasn't just a matter of settling things so Hettie would be provided for. She couldn't abide the idea of him continuing to regard her as someone, not different from who she was, but less than who she could be.

And yet there was Hettie—and Glenna. Jamey still saw it as her responsibility to care for Glenna, with her broken ankle. But eventually her mother would recover. By then, Jamey hoped to have the job as ranch hand, and she became even more determined to get that better-paying and more promising position. Then her mother would see how Jamey had worked it out: since Josh and Kit were short-termers, the old bunkhouse would be vacant with their departure, allowing Jamey to move in with Hettie. She intended to use her extra income to pay her mother or another qualified woman for onsite day care. The situation would be no different than what thousands of mothers had to deal with, working all day and caring for their children at night. And it would give Glenna more options in deciding what to do with the rest of *her* life.

She let her gaze drift to Hettie, the nipple half out of her mouth as she dozed. Jamey's earliest memories were of the redheaded man who filled the frame of her vision with his largeness of build and spirit, who carried her before him on the saddle, who taught her to rope and ride. Yet there must have been a time when she'd been babbled to and sung to and tsked at for letting no one get between her and her bottle, a time when Glenna's had been the voice or image Jamey first sought. She admired her mother for her quiet strength and her own largeness of spirit that was patient rather than forceful. Perhaps inside her there was a part of Jamey that was like her mother, inborn and inbred. Who knew? She only knew she wanted to be admired the same way by her own daughter, however that was accomplished.

So many words, so many unresolved issues remained between them, yet Jamey couldn't let them return to their dormancy without trying to make Glenna understand this about her. "Momma, I'm a cowgirl. I don't naturally know how to be a wife or mother." She sent a hand across the tabletop, to try to express not the words she couldn't say, but the ones she didn't have. "I'm not like you, I'm like Daddy. I know cattle and horses and ranching."

Glenna said nothing, her lips pressed together. Holding back words, too. Or not finding them, either. Jamey's hand closed into a fist.

Then her mother said, "No, you're not me. But you're not your daddy, either. Neither was Henry, and neither is Kell Hamilton. Don't put someone into a mold just because you don't know them or what they want, and you don't know what else do to with them. Don't put yourself into one, either."

She reached out to grasp Jamey's fingers and pull her fist open, only to close tight once more as their hands enfolded each other. And though much still remained unsaid, Jamey was reassured by her mother's touch. Abruptly she recalled how James Dunn had been determined she wouldn't leave with Henry. And Glenna's quiet command, "Let our daughter go, James."

Beyond Glenna, a man came into Jamey's view.

"God bless America!" she exclaimed, startling Glenna and Hettie. The nipple popped out of the baby's mouth as she began to wail. Jamey pulled her against her shoulder to muffle Hettie's cries, which were calling attention to the three of them.

"Oh, Momma, it's him!" she said, almost wailing herself.

"Who?" Glenna craned around.

"Don't look!" Jamey commanded, hunching her shoulders and ducking down in her seat, her hand cradling the back of Hettie's head. "It's Kell. What in tarnation is he doing *here?*"

"I could be wrong, but he might be looking for some dinner." Her mother picked up her silverware and resumed eating.

"I can't let him see me like this."

"Like what?"

"All gussied up like a champeen stud on auction day." Hettie cried more loudly at the jostling she was taking. Jamey stared at her child in horror. "I can't let him see Hettie!"

She peeked around Glenna, saw the hostess gesturing Kell to a stool at the counter, and considered herself mightily undeserving of this complication. After all, she'd been to church that very morning.

Thinking fast, she said, "All right, you take the baby."
She transferred her daughter across the table like a sack of
flour before hunkering down again. "I'll walk up front like
I just finished. I'll say hello, pass the time of day, and leave.
You wait a minute, then follow with Hettie."

"But, Jamey," Glenna reminded her, "my ankle."

Jamey was inclined to utter one of her father's oaths but
she'd never been much of a cusser, and it *was* Sunday, even
if she was feeling distinctly forsaken right now. "What am
I going to do?"

"Maybe I could finish my own dinner," Glenna suggested, "while you have a cup of coffee with Kell as he eats
his. You know, keep him distracted. When he's done, tell
him you want to visit the rest room, which will give him time
to leave, then you come back to help me with Hettie."

Jamey smiled at Glenna. "Perfect." She handed the rest
of the baby's gear across to her mother. Grabbing her
jacket, she squeezed Glenna's fingers again before slither-
ing out of the booth. "Thanks, Momma."

Glenna smiled serenely back.

Jamey strode up the aisle, wanting to be far from the in-
criminating evidence of her daughter and mother when she
"happened" upon Kell.

He'd just ordered when she passed the counter, and he
glanced up. And stared.

"Why, hello there!" Jamey declared with feigned surprise, treating Kell to a bright smile that seemed to take him
aback even more. Well, and no wonder. They'd been dancing around each other for days, ever since their argument.
And that kiss.

Kell rose, his gaze taking in her attire head to toe, and
Jamey remembered the dress she wore that did nothing to
discount her femininity. There wasn't going to be much of
a problem distracting this man, she thought cynically. Then
she remembered Glenna's mysterious smile and guessed her
mother was doing a little conspiring herself. Regardless,

Jamey couldn't suppress the surge of pleasure at the masculine appreciation in Kell's brown eyes.

"Jamey," he murmured. "Hello."

The way he spoke, soft and low, just about turned her inside out. In a pair of flats, instead of her usual boots, she really had to look up at him today, a singular experience. Remembering herself, Jamey dulled the brightness of her smile by a few watts. "Here for dinner?"

"Mmm-hmm. Care to join me?" he said as if he already knew the script to Glenna's rapidly devised plan. Jamey almost missed her cue.

"Um, sure, I'd like that. I mean, I already ate but I could have coffee or somethin'."

He smiled slowly. "Then let's see if we can get a table." Before she could protest, he'd motioned to the hostess and they were being led to a booth—right next to her mother's.

Jamey wondered how odd it would look if she excused herself to the ladies' room right now and remained there until Kell left.

When she stood rooted in indecision next to the booth, he gestured for her to have a seat, and Jamey was forced to make a quick judgment on whether to sit on the side facing Glenna's booth, or to sit back to back with her mother. She chose to face her mother and daughter.

Kell arranged for his order to be brought to the table and for an extra cup for Jamey, which he filled from the insulated carafe left by the waitress. Avoiding his gaze lest he detect her whirling thoughts, she sipped her coffee as she searched her mind madly for something to talk about, realizing that everything either of them did say would be overheard by Glenna.

Kell drank his coffee, as well. "Not as good as yours," he ventured.

She sputtered, almost dropping her cup. "My what?"

"Coffee. Yours is much better. I've gotten used to it in the morning." Jamey saw him take her in with a flicker of eyelashes. Hurriedly she dropped her gaze once more rather than deal with the sensations that look produced in her. In faded jeans and a sheepskin-lined jacket, he looked particularly wild and rugged today, especially in contrast to her attire. His once new boots had become scuffed and dusty in the past weeks, and his hair had grown down on his collar, losing that direct-from-the-barber appearance. Now it was a little longish and distractingly windblown. He hadn't shaved.

"May I say that you look pretty in that dress?" he asked.

"Sure, why not?" Jamey mumbled into her coffee cup.

"It matches your eyes. But I guess that's why you picked that color."

He seemed awfully bold today, complimenting her on her coffee and dress. But then, here she sat, shiny and ripe as a Granny Smith apple, fairly taunting Kell to indulge himself. Dismally, Jamey saw the gap widen between how he perceived her and how she wanted him to.

She remembered her mother's advice. Mentally rejected it out of hand. Then decided to try a little of it. With Glenna listening in, Jamey was certain she'd prove *her* point.

Going for a feminine gesture, Jamey drew her hair back behind her ear with one finger. Kell's eyes followed the movement, and the next, in which she let her fingers drift down her jawline and brush idly over her lower lip.

His Adam's apple lifted as he swallowed.

This was entirely too easy, she thought with a twinge of annoyance. He disappointed her. When she did get around to ranch talk, she half expected him to tell her not to worry her pretty little head about it. To which Jamey would respond by giving him a right smart crack upside of his.

Thinking it best to start on a neutral topic and wend her way around to discussing Plum Creek, she asked, "Did you come into town just for dinner?"

"Pretty much," he answered with a one-sided smile. "It's kind of quiet out there on Sundays without the usual morning bustle. Without ... you."

Despite her reservations on the wisdom of this experiment, Jamey didn't have to fake her purely female response to his softly spoken comment and frank gaze. Her cheeks filled with warmth and she got the strongest urge to bat her eyelashes. So she wasn't immune to charming smiles and flattery, either. The proof of that peeked at her over Glenna's shoulder.

"And you?" Kell asked. "Did you come into Borger to see your mother?"

She jumped. "Yes. I saw her ... earlier, and I was just about to see her again."

"I've noticed that you're quite a dutiful daughter," he said approvingly.

"Oh, I don't know about that," Jamey hastened to remark, well aware of Glenna behind Kell. She fingered her spoon. "I'm afraid I haven't been so good of one this past year."

"You mean, not being there when your father died?"

She raised her eyes and met Kell's. "Exactly."

"I'm sure you had a good reason."

"Well, I didn't," she bluntly disagreed. "I mean, I had a good reason for not bein' with him at his ... time. I didn't have a good reason for leavin' in the first place."

"I see." His eyes were filled with empathy, affecting her even more deeply than his potently sensual study of her a few minutes ago. "You shouldn't go on blaming yourself, Jamey. Like you said, what's done is done, and it's best to move on."

His food arrived, saving her from a reply. This wasn't the conversation she'd hoped to initiate, with him helping her, instead of the other way around. Still, she experienced a certain lifting of spirit, balm for her doubting soul. Such sensations, however, weren't getting her any closer to her goal.

She gave him a few minutes to dig into his meal before saying in an obvious change of subject, "So, how's everything going with getting Plum Creek back into shape?" At his strange look, she tried giving her lashes a distracting flap and hoped she didn't look as idiotic as she felt. "I'm sure you must be doin' just *wonderful* with the boys and cattle and all."

He paused in his eating, gaze clouded as his brows joined over his eyes, momentarily eclipsing them. "It's coming along," he said cautiously, dimming Jamey's hopes even as she grew relieved. She actually preferred this Kell, who wouldn't be deterred from his purpose by a comely face and manner, and wouldn't make it his purpose in life to pursue them, either—as Henry had. Which got Jamey thinking that this just wasn't going to work. Perhaps, as Glenna had pointed out, she hid the real Jamey Dunn from Kell, but this Gentle Miss wasn't her, either. She wanted Kell to like and respect her for *her*.

Still, she tried another smile, stalling, as she searched for a way to get him talking about the workings on the ranch so she could do as her mother had suggested and "offer" her advice. She was painfully aware that Glenna was party to her awkwardness.

"I was wonderin'," she finally said, "about that little roan mare with the white star on her forehead."

"You mean Rosie?"

Jamey smiled spontaneously, liking the name. "Yes, Rosie. I've gone out to look at her when I've had some free time. How come you and the boys don't use her, trade her off with one of the other horses?" Jamey already knew the answer to this question but was trying her best to be subtle. She hoped she didn't appear dumber than dirt.

"She's not trained, not completely," Kell responded. "Whatever she's learned, she's forgotten with disuse." He leaned back, stretching his arm out along the back of the booth, and sipped his coffee. "She's half Arabian, half quarter horse. Sturdy enough, but excitable. A real wild one, and getting wilder by the day without something to do. I don't know what Bud intended to use her for. Breeding, maybe. I haven't decided what to do with her myself."

"She's got good conformation," Jamey said, making her tone ruminative, as Kell's was. Just a friendly, nonconfrontational chat. "Close coupled, which makes for a good cow horse. I bet she can turn on a dime."

"Maybe. She's unpredictable, though, from what I've seen. Can't be counted on to hold her ground."

"But as a breed, Arabians have more endurance than quarter horses. They're usually smart, too, with a lot of heart." She paused as if in contemplation. "Wouldn't it be...interesting to see what Rosie could do with a little time and training?"

The suggestion was as indirect as she could make it, and yet Kell's gaze homed in on hers. She looked back with an appeal she simply couldn't hide, getting that desperate feeling again. "I wouldn't neglect my other chores at all. I promise."

"It's not that—"

"And I won't...I won't even hint at bein' a ranch hand. That's what you're thinking this is all about, aren't you? To show you what I can do."

He arched a brow. "Are you telling me it's not?"

"It might've been before, but now...I feel like *I've* got to be doin' something, too. Something I'm good at. Something I love."

Kell set down his coffee cup. "Jamey," he said, his mouth open to say more. However he closed it again, apparently thinking better of whatever impulse he'd had. Yet he seemed to inwardly debate the matter. She waited, her heart in her eyes.

Finally he said, "I understand how you feel, Jamey. I really do. But Rosie is quite a handful. You'd be alone with her in the corral with no help if an emergency came up."

"Josh and Kit are almost always within shouting distance."

"Yes, but—" His eyes roamed her features. "You're my responsibility, and I don't want you getting hurt."

Her thoughts scattered. That gaze could put a shine on a rusty trailer hitch. Then she shook her head. Confound it, he was being protective again! He *had* to stop seeing her as a woman. And she had to stop wanting him to.

This time, though, she didn't deny her womanhood, wouldn't accuse him of discriminating against her for it. "Kell, I'd be careful. I'm good with horses. Trust me on that. Besides, Rosie deserves a chance to show people what she can do. Doesn't she?" Jamey remembered her mother's suggestion to offer advice, instead of tell him what he ought to do, and came up with a turn on that approach that was all hers, one she could get behind. She'd still say, direct and forthright, what was on her mind and what she wanted—but she'd ask him for it.

"May I try my hand at training Rosie, Kell?" she asked softly, which always made her husky voice huskier. Intentionally or not, if he'd likened her to the independent Brahman before, then Jamey was definitely making a plea for herself now through Rosie. "Please?"

She waited on tenterhooks as Kell broke eye contact first, tipping his head back on his neck and taking a deep breath. She saw his Adam's apple do another bob in his muscled, stubble-shadowed throat. No, she didn't have a natural instinct about men, but something told Jamey that Kell was going to say yes, give her a chance. And she was glad she'd come by it honestly.

Then, behind him, she noticed Hettie, eyes slightly crossed as she focused on her target—which was the top of Kell's head.

"Het—" Jamey cut off her yelp and watched helplessly as the baby clutched a hank of hair and pulled.

Kell made a sound of surprised pain as he reached back and caught the baby's wrist, not roughly, just to keep it still so she wouldn't pull any harder.

"Hettie!" Glenna admonished as she turned around, snatching Hettie's hand and disengaging damp fingers from Kell's hair. The baby came away with several brown strands trapped in her fist. Glenna met Jamey's eyes, which widened in urgency as Jamey jerked her head in a covert command to get her mother to turn back around before Kell got a view of her. Not that he'd recognize her mother, having never met her, but the two of them—Jamey and Glenna—were already pushing it.

Glenna averted her face as Kell pivoted, rubbing his scalp, to get a look at his assailant. He didn't appear annoyed.

"I'm sorry, sir," Glenna mumbled, lowering her chin so her hair hid her features. "She's at the stage where she tries to grab everything she sees."

"No trouble, ma'am," Kell told her. "Reminds me that I need a haircut."

Her chin sank lower, buried in the baby's nape. "Yessir."

Kell gave Glenna a puzzled glance. Hettie, on the other hand, stared at him boldly, mesmerized by his deep voice. "You've got a cute baby there, ma'am," he complimented her as Jamey encountered a dismaying emotion very close to rivalry. Hettie was *her* baby.

"Th-thank you," Glenna replied.

Kell smiled at the child. "Hello," he said—in the exact tone he'd said the same word to Jamey not ten minutes before.

Hettie's forehead wrinkled, and she looked almost ready to cry. Then she gave Kell a big, drooly, gurgly, flirty, toothless grin. And shoved her fist in her mouth in sheer delight.

Laughing, Kell turned back around, and every petty thought fled from Jamey's head. His brown eyes were lit with melting warmth and enchantment, his face open and tender, all because of a baby's smile. *Her* baby's smile.

Oh, my heavens, was all she could think. A stirring started way down inside, an involuntary reaction to this man. Her vision blurred around the edges and her focus sharpened. If there was something in men's genes that made them pursue the female sex, looking to sow their seed, then there was an equally powerful force in women, making them want to appear the most attractive to the male who'd best provide for and protect her and her young. It was part of the mating dance, Jamey realized, that circling of one another, assessing, evaluating. Courting.

Suddenly she wanted to tell Kell that Hettie was hers, that she'd borne a child and could bear more. She wanted to list, bluntly and brazenly, all the qualities that would make her a desirable mate. *A good wife,* she thought, surprising herself.

"Looks like she could just about charm the pants off of you, doesn't she?" Kell remarked.

"Takes after her father, I'd wager," she replied without rancor. "She *is* darlin', isn't she?" Jamey beamed her approval at Hettie. "Momma says it's God's plan, making babies cute, otherwise you'd be hard pressed to put up with them bein' babies."

Kell chuckled. His own expression seemed lit from within. "Do you want children, Jamey?"

It was as if he already knew what she'd been thinking. "I'd have a dozen if I could," she said fervently.

His eyes became hooded. Assessing. "Somehow I think you'd make a good mother."

"You do?"

"Sure. From what I've seen, you've got a lot of self-discipline and stick-to-itiveness. I've seen your loyalty to your family, your protectiveness. I think you'd see to your

kids' welfare no matter the odds against you. You're con-
scientious and responsible that way."

Admirable qualities all, Jamey thought, and none of them
uniquely associated with the feminine sex. She felt more
flattered than when he'd complimented her dress.

"Well," she demurred, "it's sure I'll never be good at all
the things my mother did for me, like sewing and baking
cookies."

"I think it's more important people feel they're doing
something worthwhile with their lives, be happy with themselves, that makes them a better person, and so a better
parent."

"I agree. I—I'm tryin' to do that, you know," she said
quietly. "To be a better person, I mean."

"I know, Jamey. So am I."

His eyes weren't just brown, Jamey thought as she stared
into them. They were deep, textured and as complex as the
nap on velvet, or the strong coffee she brewed each morning. And like some swirling, potent liquid, she could have
easily drowned in those eyes. At their corners were tiny
lines—not laugh lines, but squint lines, worry lines, a result
of looking from horseback out across plains dotted with
cattle. She knew about such lines because she'd seen them
before—around her father's eyes.

She wanted to blurt out everything—about her father and
Henry and Hettie. Her deepest wishes and deepest fears. She
wanted to know Kell's, too, because she sensed she had before her a rare breed of man, one who might talk—*could*
talk—about such things with a woman.

But not here, not now, with Glenna listening. Not when
some of the subjects Jamey needed to talk about involved
those she couldn't bring up to her mother. Not when it was
as plain as day that Jamey was doing what she'd vowed not
to.

Kell shifted in his seat, bringing her back from her
thoughts. She realized she must have been sitting in silence

for some time, for he said formally, "Seems I've pried again."

She couldn't meet his eyes. "No, it wasn't that. I just...I need to get back. My mother's waiting."

He glanced at his watch. "And I've kept you from her." Rising, Kell picked up the bill and nodded toward the café entrance. "Walk you out?"

"No...no, I'd like to use the ladies' room," she said, falling back on the plan. "So—can I train Rosie in my spare time?" He'd never really said she could, and that was her real purpose, or should have been her real purpose, in talking to him.

He hesitated, then nodded. "If you want to try your hand with her, go ahead. Just...be careful."

"I will. When it comes to horses and cows, I'm always on my toes."

When it came to men, she was not, apparently. She watched him walk away, reaching into the back pocket of his well-fitting jeans for his billfold. The simple action left her dry-mouthed. She mentally reviewed her conversation with Kell—and knew her mother had proved her point, several of them. Kell wouldn't fit into a mold. He was unique. And Jamey *was* interested in him, incredibly tempted to give in to the impulse to fall for him. She'd nearly forgotten her goal, had as much as promised him she'd stop pursuing it, and she had to wonder why. Was it because she needed so badly to be doing something she was good at? Or had she given up on doing a cowboy's job because it *would* solve so many problems for her to stay on as cook?

Uncertainty and guilt engulfed her as Jamey wondered at the best course: to try for the job that fulfilled her and made her a better person for her daughter, or to settle for the one that would allow Jamey to take responsibility, truly, for the baby she'd borne. To be a real mother to Hettie.

Was that the real reason she found Kell so attractive?

She didn't know. She'd never figured out, either, what impulse it was that had made her fall for and ultimately marry Henry. It struck her that Henry and she had never really talked person to person as she and Kell did. Henry had said pretty words and phrases that she realized now never actually meant anything. He'd just taken control from the beginning, and she'd never thought it could be different. As her mother had said, he'd led the dance, literally. That was how they'd met. Henry had asked her, she'd said she didn't know how, and he'd said not to worry, he would take care of her. And he had. Being in his arms was like nothing she'd experienced before. She hadn't known the two-step from the Cotton-Eyed Joe, yet Henry had swung her around the sawdusted dance floor so smoothly it was as if she'd been waltzing all her life. She could have gone on dancing for—

Did you really think it'd last forever?

Her gaze continued to follow Kell's form outside as he headed for his pickup, bracing himself against the biting February wind. It was so strong and bitter, the saying went, because nothing lay between the Panhandle and the North Pole except a "ba'b" wire fence—and that was down. It took a certain kind of man to make ranching work here. Jamey wanted Kell to fulfill that goal. But she couldn't repeat her mistakes with another cowboy. Whatever need within her that had yet to be fulfilled, she needed to fill it herself.

She had a feeling, though, that the mating dance had already begun.

Chapter Six

Jamey took another trip to the back door and peered into the black winter evening, seeing nothing as she'd seen nothing the dozen times she'd stared out there before. Behind her, the boys wolfed down supper like there was no tomorrow, as was their habit. End-of-the-day chats came after satisfying appetites made sharp by hard work and cold weather. Her own appetite was dulled by worry. Kell had yet to return for the evening. Any number of accidents that might have occurred plagued her.

"The boss is sure to be in soon, Miss Jamey," Charley called from behind her, quaintly gracious, as always, in a way that touched her. "He's often the last one in of an evening."

She turned from her vigil and gave the grizzled cowboy a grateful smile that turned his milk jug ears as red as his windburned face. "Yes, but each time he's told one of you what would keep him."

No, it wasn't unusual for Kell to make it in after the others, though he'd never been this late before, nor, as she'd pointed out, without seeing one of the boys and mentioning his purpose. He seemed to be working extra hard these days, she reflected. She'd seen the light on under the office door on more than a few occasions when, late into the evening, she'd returned to the main house for one reason or another. After their conversation at the restaurant a few weeks ago, she'd tried not to care what he was going through, but then she'd think of her father and what had happened to him, and how it seemed Kell was wearing himself out, too. Her stomach churned with sheer apprehension as her own concerns faded. She wanted to scold him, tell him he couldn't continue taking on so much responsibility. Yet the alternative might be that he'd decide his aim to make it as a rancher was futile—and let Plum Creek go.

She couldn't let him do that, either.

"I seen the boss this afternoon afore he sent Kit and me over to give Purdy a hand with that windmill that's broke in the west section," Josh volunteered. "He said he was going to take a look at the north fence and see what damage the Hell Cow done to it." The boys had taken to calling the Brahman by name, a bad sign in Jamey's opinion. It meant things had gotten personal between the Brahman and the cowboys. She'd certainly seen how Kell reacted to incidents involving the cow.

Jamey was unaware of how worried she must have looked until Purdy piped up, "If the boss ain't back by the time we're finished here, Josh and me'll go lookin' for him." She knew they weren't unconcerned for their employer, only that a hasty reaction of jumping in the pickup and going in search of Kell before he was barely missed would be viewed as a lack of confidence in him. In other words, Kell was a big cowboy and it should be assumed that he could take care of himself. Just because Jamey had some tender feelings for Kell that made her react as a woman didn't mean she couldn't see the merit in that course of action.

So she swallowed her impatience and, with another smile, said, "Thanks, Purdy."

Despite Kell's misgivings about how she would get along with the boys, and vice versa, Jamey found herself easier with them than with Kell. They seemed to accept her for herself, as she accepted each of them as individuals. Purdy treated her like a daughter, Charley was her gallant knight, and Josh and Kit . . . well, they'd certainly seemed at first to have designs on her, but that had mysteriously changed within a few days, and now they were quite brotherly toward her. She couldn't shake the hunch that the change in attitude had less to do with her baggy clothes than with Kell—and some unacknowledged claim on her. On the one hand she was glad not to have to deal with the problem; on the other, it rankled her to think the boys considered her Kell's.

Jamey wondered if the boys' attitudes would mirror Kell's once they knew she wanted to do their job. She may have promised, of a fashion, to set aside seeking the ranch hand position, but she hadn't given up on that goal. She couldn't let herself do that, either.

The muffled slam of the mudroom door met her ears. A few seconds later Kell entered the kitchen, stopping at the sight of her, hands on her hips.

"There you are!" Jamey said, unable to keep relief from her voice. She stood directly in Kell's path, and he hesitated, his face lined with exhaustion.

"Sorry I'm late," he apologized shortly.

Even realizing she'd overreacted, Jamey wanted to scold him, motherlike, the way she'd held back for days from doing. Yet she had no right to, and besides, the boys were looking on. So she took to scolding him another way. "The stew's still warm, but the muffins are stone cold. I'll have to heat them up in the oven and it'll dry 'em out," she said, aware that she sounded not like a worried mother but a shrewish housewife, which irritated her even more. She managed to refrain from making a comment about slaving over a hot stove all day.

"Don't bother," Kell said. "I'm not very hungry right now."

"Oh, it's no *bother*," she returned. His brown eyes grew as frosty as the weather outside at her tone. Something told her she should quit now and leave well enough alone. She'd been careful in her dealings with him since that day in the restaurant, careful to keep her distance lest the urges she felt so strongly overcame her better judgment. But there was a particular air of discouragement about him tonight, and she recalled her observations of him working too hard. He couldn't miss too many meals or he'd get worn down. He couldn't give up! "A cowboy not bein' hungry after a day in the saddle?" she scoffed. "That's a new one."

His mouth thinned. "Well, *this* cowboy isn't. I'll find something to eat later if I want it." With that, he brushed past her, continuing through the kitchen to the back of the house. From behind him, she saw he walked slowly and gingerly, like a man with boot-tender bare feet going across gravel.

Jamey stared after him, then sent her gaze around the table of ranch hands. To a man, they tucked their chins, avoiding her eyes, and shoveled huge mouthfuls of apple pan dowdy down their gullets with what she thought was vast indifference.

"Somethin's going on here, and I intend to find out what it is," she announced.

"I wouldn't do that, Jamey," Purdy said without looking up.

Jamey opened her mouth, a tart response on the tip of her tongue, then closed it again. The message was loud and clear: if they saw no reason to push the subject, she shouldn't, either.

Still, she couldn't let go of her worry. After the hands had retired to their quarters, leaving her to clean up, Jamey

continued to wonder what was up with Kell. Remaining in
the main house well past nine o'clock, ostensibly to do
laundry, she waited for him to return to the kitchen. He had
to be hungry. She considered taking a tray to him in his
bedroom, where she'd determined he was, but the gesture
stuck in her craw after the way he'd rejected her meal earlier.

Still, nothing allayed the nagging sense of something being wrong, and so at ten o'clock, long after she would have
been in bed, Jamey silently walked down the darkened hall
to Kell's bedroom. She clutched a stack of folded clothes in
her arms as her reason for being there.

Yet before she reached his door, the one farther down the
hallway opened, and Kell, shirtless and wearing only a pair
of jeans slung low on his hips, stepped out of the bathroom. He'd obviously just showered or bathed, for his hair
was wet.

He caught sight of her.

"I have some towels to put away," Jamey explained
breathlessly. His shoulders seemed even broader without his
shirt, perhaps because his fully revealed torso narrowed toward the waist into a sharp, perfect V. With the light from
the bathroom casting shadows on the planes of his face and
chest, he looked like a statue, she decided, wonderfully de-
tailed—and motionless as if truly carved in stone. She'd
never seen such a cold expression on his face.

"Kell, is something wrong?" she asked, not caring if she
was personal with him. She wanted to help. She had to help,
as if this really was her chance to rewrite the past and prevent Kell from suffering a fate similar to her father's—not
one of losing his life, but of losing his faith in himself. Yet
that had more to do with how she felt about herself than her
father.

"Go to bed, Jamey," he said.

She took a step forward. "No, there's something wrong." Then she saw what the shadows had hidden. Along one side of his ribcage was a large, ugly, deep purple bruise.

Kell saw Jamey's eyes widen and knew what she'd spotted. Part of him didn't care. He was so damned tired tonight. Tired of it all.

"You're hurt!" she cried, rushing to him, her arm extended.

He raised a hand to keep her from coming any closer. Even that small but abrupt movement made him wince. He ached all over, and the thought of someone touching him right now, even Jamey, had the appeal of placing a hot brand on his skin.

"I'm fine," he lied. "It's nothing serious."

"Let me see!" she said with no indication of having heard him. With her free hand she took his elbow and turned him toward better light as she bent to peer at his side. "What in heaven's name happened—" She cut herself off, and Kell knew it was because she'd discerned the imprint of a hoof in his skin that he'd just thoroughly examined in the bathroom mirror. The answer to her question was obvious: he'd gotten stomped.

"No broken skin, at least. I bet that hurts like a bear." She glanced up at him with pure sympathy in her gray-green eyes. Sympathy he didn't want or deserve.

"I've been soaking in a hot tub for an hour and I feel fine. Now if you'll let me by—"

"You don't look fine. And this looks like a couple of cracked ribs."

"They're just bruised. It's not like I punctured a lung," he remarked, unable to keep the sarcasm from his voice.

"Mumph," she said, meaning she'd see for herself. "Where else are you hurt?"

"It'd take a lot less time to tell you where I'm not," he shot back, done with the inquisition. He hoped she'd let the subject drop and not ask any more questions, but it wasn't to be.

"Do you want to tell me what happened?" she asked.

"Not particularly." He noticed how she tactfully rephrased her earlier inquiry, but it didn't diminish his annoyance as he tried not to recoil from her like an injured animal as she skimmed a finger over the imprint with the lightest of touches. That grazing contact didn't smart like he'd thought it would, but it didn't feel...good, either. Then she palpated the spot, still with gentle fingers. He couldn't prevent sucking in a breath, which expanded his chest and caused another spasm of pain to shoot through his injured muscles. Gripping the nearby doorjamb, Kell bit off a curse.

"Why not?" she asked, still probing delicately.

"Because," he said through gritted teeth, "I don't want to hear what is bound to be one of your blunt-as-you-please opinions on how it served me right to get in a wreck with that infernal, blasted, damn-it-to-hell Brahman cow. Now will you let me by so I can go lick my wounds in peace?"

She raised her brows like a disapproving mother, and he guessed he was seeing the Jamey Dunn who knew how to handle cowboys, as she'd claimed. Except today he'd not proved himself to be much of one.

"Nothin' seems to be wrong with your mouth," she observed wryly. "And I'll bet your pride is what smarts most right now, which you'll be glad to learn no one's ever died of." She straightened and looked him in the eye, which with him barefoot and her in boots, she could do handily. "I don't suppose there's any way you'd drive into Borger and get that X-rayed."

"I don't suppose there's any way you'd butt out of my business," he countered sourly.

"I didn't think so. All right, you get on into the bedroom and lay down," she instructed. "I'll be in after I've gone through the bathroom cabinet to see what your uncle left you by way of medicines."

He would have protested her ordering him around, but it just so happened he was heading to bed, anyway. Trying not to actually hobble, Kell walked to his bedroom and slowly, painfully, eased himself down on the quilted spread. He stared at the ceiling.

Never in his life had he been more frustrated. It wasn't so much the fall he'd taken today as the accumulation of defeats and hindrances that had been building up over the past month and a half. Josh and Kit had been putting patches on top of patches in repairing the buildings, but it looked like the barn definitely would need a new roof. He'd been out to see the old windmill Purdy and Charley had been working on, and it needed a major overhaul, too. Kell knew his uncle had resisted going the modern route and replacing the windmills with submergible pumps, but he was ready to admit Bud had taken tradition to the extreme. The next big expense, Kell decided, would be replacing the windmills with pumps, but for now they'd have to make do.

Then there was the inventory, a nebulous process. Purdy and Charley estimated the total number of pregnant cows to be at least ten percent lower than what he'd planned, meaning Kell could scarcely stand to lose even one calf this spring. Which also meant it would make little sense to put wheels under the pregnant Brahman just to get her out of his life.

This environment wasn't just rough, he decided, it was downright hostile. He wondered how Bud had ever made a living here, wondered what reward would ever make it worth the hardship.

Wondered if he'd made a mistake committing to Plum Creek.

Jamey entered the room carrying a variety of tubes, bottles and an Ace bandage. Setting them on the nightstand, she settled on the edge of the bed next to him. She took a minute to study the labels on each container, and the light from the bedside lamp cast a warm glow on her fine skin and vibrant red hair. Great, why not put himself through a little more torture right now? Though he knew Jamey cleaned his room, changed the bed and even put his clothes away, he'd never actually been in the bedroom with her here. The intimacy of her presence stirred him—at the one time when he had the least ability to do something about it.

Just as well. It had disturbed him to learn she'd taken a job here to convince him what a good cowpuncher she could be, when he'd been harboring sentiments of her wanting to help him for nobler reasons. And so tonight he was less than willing to have her see *him* as less than competent. Yet he had an idea the damage had already been done. The fact that she sat on the edge of his bed without a thought to discretion reinforced that assumption. Actually, over the past few weeks she'd already distanced herself from him, which also bothered him even while he concluded it was for the best that she had.

Yet right now she seemed approachable, tender, nurturing. And it made him doubt she'd be able to handle some of the more ruthless ranch duties he knew she still pined to do, even though she seemed to have given up convincing him of that. Truthfully, though, Kell knew his own problem handling the job influenced his doubts about Jamey as a full-time ranch hand. The altercation with the Hell Cow today had served to put a head on this discouragement, which had been brewing in him for weeks.

Kell hadn't even realized he'd tensed until he heard Jamey's gentle admonishment, her hand on his arm. "Try to relax. It's going to hurt no matter what. Have you taken any of these, yet?" She showed him the bottle of an over-the-counter anti-inflammatory.

"I took one about an hour ago."

"Here, take another, it won't hurt you." She provided him with a tablet and a glass of water, as he stifled a wince and rose up on one elbow to wash the pill down. He felt like a damned newborn.

Jamey squeezed a dollop of white salve from a tube and proceeded to apply it to his side, although she avoided the bruise itself. Elbow pointed skyward to keep his arm out of her way, Kell pinched the bridge of his nose. The ointment felt cool on his skin at first, but after a few moments it began to grow hot and sting. Like a bear.

"Son of a... what is that stuff?"

"A liniment for sore muscles. The menthol makes it sting." She continued smoothing the cream into his skin with incredibly gentle strokes. "So," she said after some time had passed in which Kell actually began to loosen up under her ministrations, "the Brahman's up to her old tricks."

"Is she ever." He snorted in pure exasperation. "It wouldn't be a problem if it was just her going down into that washout, but she always takes a few heifers with her. And some of those pregnant cows aren't able to get out. I'd go ahead with my original thinking and build a fence around it, but we're getting behind on other jobs that just can't wait. When it comes right down to it, I don't want to spend money on fencing materials if I don't absolutely have to. And you were right when you said the place would draw coyote or cougar. I've seen footprints. With birthing time nearing, it's courting danger to let any of the heifers follow the Brahman down there."

"If the Brahman's the only one with a bent for wanderin' into the washout, why not pen her up here in the corral until after the calves hit the ground?"

"I'd rather make hamburger out of her," Kell replied with acrimony as he rested a forearm over his closed eyes. "She's the most stubborn, irritating, maddening creature I've ever known."

Jamey chuckled. He sneaked a peek at her from under his wrist. Her head was bent as she industriously nursed his injury. With her eyes downcast, he had the opportunity to note once more how long her lashes were. In this light they were gold-tipped. He'd bet they were as soft as a sable brush. She bit her lower lip between her teeth as he'd noticed was her habit when concentrating. Her features held an almost indefinable aspect—one of sensitivity and caring. She looked feminine and downright alluring. Not for the first time, he thought of how this side of Jamey spoke to the deepest part of him.

"Turn over and let me do your back before I wrap your ribs with this bandage," Jamey said.

Obediently, Kell turned over as he noted that his aches were beginning to lessen. He buried his hands under the pillow that he sank his head onto and gave himself over to the pleasure of being nursed by her. There was certainly something about having a woman fussing over him that appeased any number of ills.

"Mmm," she murmured as her hands worked their magic on him, "you've got some nasty-looking bruises back here, too."

"Feels like it," he grunted as she found a particularly sore spot. But the last thing he wanted her to do was stop.

"I don't mean to poke my nose into your business, Kell, but if you'd like to tell me how this happened..." She ran the tips of her fingers down his spine, neck to waist, as if to physically soothe his bruised ego as she soothed his bruised body. "I promise I won't lecture you."

Lulled by her throaty voice, Kell sighed. He might as well tell her. "Like I said, the Brahman was in that sinkhole with a heifer coming up on her first calving. I drove the heifer out easy enough, but that Brahman wouldn't budge." He could feel himself getting irritated again. "Nope, she headed right for this thorny thicket of wild plum when she saw me. That'll tell you how contrary she is. If she got into that, I knew I'd never get her out. Not that I needed to. The other heifer was safe, and God knows the Brahman could take care of herself. But the thought of her standing in that copse staring out at me and knowing she'd won... Somehow I managed to get a throw off and drop a loop over her neck, pulling her up just short of her mark, which only made her more ornery. And..."

"And?"

"Why I threw that rope, or what I thought I'd do if I caught her, I don't know," he muttered into the pillow, glad he faced away from Jamey, because next was the embarrassing part. "She just made me so damn mad. And I must've made *her* mad, because she swapped ends—as Purdy would say—and charged straight for me and my horse. I did the only thing I could think of and spurred Gringo forward, out of the cow's direct path, and she swept past us—taking the rope right under Gringo's tail."

"Oh," Jamey said, and the word spoke volumes.

"Yeah, oh. Gringo boiled up and went berserk." His mind pictured the image, almost from an outsider's point of view, of the buckskin rearing, him hanging on to the saddle horn for dear life, and the Brahman's wide hind end loping away from him. He'd realized what was bound to happen and that he was virtually helpless to prevent it. Suddenly he understood why cowboys laughed at a buddy getting into a wreck. In a way, it looked funny, and by laughing, they could avoid thinking about how close one of them had come to critical injury, or that they faced that danger every day. "I might've had a chance if the Hell Cow hadn't run out of rope at the exact moment I was setting myself for Gringo to rear one way and the rope jerked him the other."

"So down you went."

"Like a ton of lead. I hit the ground flat on my back, knocking the wind out of me. I looked up and saw hooves pawing the air right above me. I scrambled out of the way of the front feet but Gringo tread on me with a sidestep on his hind foot."

"You're lucky. If he'd come down on you with his front hooves—" Her hand paused in midstroke, palm resting on his back, this time as if to reassure herself rather than him.

Yet she asked calmly, "What happened to Gringo and the Brahman?"

"The horse was spooked, I was on the ground—there was no way I could expect to climb aboard and finish what I'd started. Someone would get hurt. So I cut the rope," Kell said, knowing he'd just admitted to Jamey the breadth of his incompetence. Cutting your rope was equivalent to getting a client's transaction wrong in the investment management business. Not irrecoverable, but it sure set back a person's faith in your capabilities. He almost wished Jamey *would* find the incident funny, or go ahead and lecture him.

She did neither as she said, very softly, "So the home-end of the rope was tied solid to your saddle horn."

"Yes," Kell replied, wondering at her question. "That's how I rope. That's how Bud roped," he corrected. "He taught me."

"Well, I can see how it'd be a matter of pri—habit—to tie hard and fast, especially for your uncle. It's a time-honored and perfectly reasonable ropin' technique. Works just fine on flat ground with a normal cow." *Or if you know what you're doing,* Kell heard her leave out. "Rodeo cowboys tie off when they're roping stock in competition, but that's just for show. No workin' cowboy would jerk a calf off its feet like the rodeo guys do. If there's a doubt about the land, or cattle, or even the horse, it's better to dally the rope 'round the horn. Most real cowboys dally, instead of tying off these days. It's safer, less risky, because if you need to, you can let the rope go in a tight spot."

"Like today."

"Kell—" She hesitated, and he sensed her searching carefully for her words. "There's no shame in getting bucked off a horse or losin' a tussle with a cow. It happens to the best of cowboys. Once, my father was dragged a good fifty yards by a steer when he—my daddy, that is—got his ankle caught in a rope. Tore up his best shirt. Momma dug rocks and dirt out of his back for months. I never saw him so spittin' mad."

"I'll bet." Kell turned his head on the pillow so he could see her. This was how it had been as they'd sat and talked in that restaurant in Borger. And he supposed he'd started to feel deeper emotions for Jamey because of the connection they'd begun to form then, the sharing of self that bonded two people together almost as surely as a physical link. Sure, they still had their differences, but he'd seen how sensitive she could be, with a great capacity for caring—although he'd seen that quality before. Watching her in the amber light, he decided that he'd been right. She *would* make a good mother, with both the intuition and strength of character needed for such a challenge. "What'd your dad do about it?"

"Well, each spring Daddy always separated one beef from the herd and penned it, feedin' it on corn and oats to fatten it up for the family's personal . . . enjoyment."

"I take it you're not talking about putting a straw hat on Bessie for kids to take their picture with the pet cow."

"No." She smiled, eyes soft as they focused on the past. "Many an evening I saw him out by the pen, talking to that steer, sweet as you please, coaxing it to eat just a little more corn. And that winter, I never saw Daddy relish a steak more."

"I like your father's approach. Maybe I *will* make hamburger out of that Brahman."

"Nothin' like the smell of barbecue to make your tummy stand up and say howdy." Jamey exaggerated her twang.

Half his face still buried in the pillow, Kell peeked at Jamey with one eye, she looked back at him, and their senses of humor took over. Then he groaned. "Ouch. It hurts to laugh."

"Hurts less than frettin' about what's happened and can't be changed, doesn't it?"

"Yeah." He peered up at her. "You've fretted about your father, haven't you, Jamey?" he said, now serious.

Nodding, Jamey became solemn, too. "I'm just beginnin' to be able to remember the good times."

"I'm glad. Your dad sounds like some kind of cowboy."

"He was . . . the best."

A blind man could have seen how Jamey set quite a store by her father. Kell wondered, just as he wondered if he had the innate talent that would allow him to excel as a cowboy, if he had the qualities that could inspire that kind of love and respect. If genes were the deciding factor, it could go either way; while his own parents weren't the best, Uncle Bud had known how to foster a child's spirit, even if he'd never had children of his own.

Perhaps that was what touched him so deeply about Jamey. He saw her searching, wanting, needing—had since the beginning, when she'd stepped into his house in that beat-up hat. He'd seen himself as a boy, forsaken by his own mother and father, and so very needful of whatever love his grizzled uncle could give him.

Even now, he couldn't prevent a sympathetic smile. "You said someday you'd tell me what happened with you and your father. I'd really like to hear it."

"Maybe." Jamey intently examined his back, avoiding his eyes. "You're . . . easy to talk to, Kell."

"For a man?" he added, trying for a lighter tone since this subject seemed to bother her, and because he really felt that that was her unspoken postscript to her statement.

Her lashes lifted and she said simply, "For a cowboy."

The air suspended in his chest, not to control the pain, but to hold the moment. It came to him that he'd been afraid he'd damage what regard Jamey had for him in revealing his roping accident. It seemed he hadn't. He supposed he was a different sort of man from those she knew all her life. Yet it was his way to talk problems or possible solutions through. And Kell realized he needed that. None of the ranch hands could be called talkative. The times he'd tried to solicit their input, he'd gotten the impression they were uncomfortable. They hadn't signed on for that kind of responsibility, just to do their jobs and draw their wages.

And then there was Jamey, ready, willing and able to help, just as he wanted to help her.

At that moment, Kell knew he wanted something quite different than to prove to Jamey—or himself—that he could be a cowboy like her father or Bud Hamilton. Because he could never be them. He could only be himself, and he needed Jamey to fill the hole in him that had been created long ago by a mother and father whose neglect had made a seven-year-old child believe that who he was was not enough to hold their love.

She'd stopped tending his injuries while the two of them talked, but now resumed them with renewed vigor.

"That Brahman definitely left her mark on you," she said, "even if she wasn't the one doing the stomping."

"It works both ways," Kell replied with his eyes closed, strangely at peace.

"You know, you could auction her, get a decent price for her, considering she's heavy bred right now and a proven producer. And you could likely replace her that very day with a different pregnant cow, and not lose a calf prospect."

"I'm tempted to, but—I think I'll keep her around for a while longer. Somehow, selling the Brahman would seem like giving up on something I'm not ready to give up on, yet. Maybe I'm being stubborn as the Hell Cow, but I'm not giving up."

Her hands continued smoothing over his back in a circular rhythm, yet her touch changed—or maybe something changed in his response. Now it felt as if the massaging had turned to... caresses. He wasn't imagining it. Every muscle in his body, once relieved of its aches and pains, responded to the slow burn in him. It didn't help when Jamey asked him to raise up on his elbows to wrap the elastic bandage around his ribs. Every time she passed the roll under him, her breasts came into brushing contact with his back. Head dropped between his shoulders, Kell reminded himself that Jamey was here on an errand of mercy and he'd be a dirty dog to take advantage of her. For weeks he'd managed not to—except for those times when she'd challenged him. Those instances disturbed him, for he knew he very nearly couldn't have stopped himself. So he focused on the higher connection they'd achieved. "It helps me to talk to you, too, Jamey."

Her fingers brushed his ribcage on their way around, not exactly tickling, but not calming, either. "I was afraid, you know," she said from behind him. "Afraid for... that you wouldn't find ranching worth it."

"Well, I'm not sure if I do," he answered, finding it hard to keep his mind on the subject. "But I'm not ready to throw in the towel just yet."

"I'm glad, Kell." Her breath was warm on his neck as she finished winding the bandage around him. He wondered if she'd any idea of her effect on him, and guessed she must not. He was relieved when she fastened the end of the bandage and he was able to ease back facedown onto the bed, hiding his physical reaction.

Then he felt something strange. She was still touching him, but it was a fingertip here, above his bandage, and there, below it, in no discernible pattern. Within seconds he found himself on a crest of anticipation that heated his blood even more as he waited to feel where next that brief contact would land.

"What are you doing?" he finally asked hoarsely.

"Countin'." Her voice was husky and low and... mesmerized. "You've got these dark freckles all over your back. There's one here, and here. And here." She pressed the pad of her finger to a spot in the small of his back, just above the waistband of his jeans. He didn't have to see it to know that was where she pointed. Her touch fairly singed his skin.

She really was an innocent if she didn't expect him to react.

"Jamey," he managed to croak out in warning.

"Eleven."

"Jamey—" Oblivious to the pain the movement produced, Kell came up on one elbow, turning toward Jamey and grabbing her wrist. Their gazes met. "I think it would be best if you left."

"I know." She didn't move.

"Go. Now."

"All right." Neither of them stirred. Then slowly, his fingers still wrapped around her wrist, Kell leaned backward as she leaned forward, as if a foot-long wire stretched between them. There *was* a connection, tangible and strong. It tugged at them both, had been pulling at them for weeks, since the moment they'd laid eyes on each other. And as Kell settled back onto the bed, he brought her close enough to touch his mouth to hers.

She had such incredible lips, lush and full and soft. She gave them to him willingly, though her mouth remained closed. Kell fought back impatience as she braced herself over him and he plied the crease between her lips with moist kisses.

She's inexperienced, his inner voice reminded him. Proof of that was in the way she kissed. He *would* be a cur to take advantage of her. But he had to have more. Framing her face with his hands, he pulled back slightly. Her gray-green eyes were as cloudy as a tidal pool, glazed over with the same desire that was making his heart thud as if he'd run a mile. With the pad of one thumb, he traced the length of her glistening lower lip, then back to its center, where he drew it downward, exposing her even white teeth. He raised his brows in question. She blinked, and he read uncertainty in her eyes—from kissing him at all? Or perhaps uncertain of what he asked of her.

So he told her. "Please," he whispered, "open up to me, Jamey. I need this."

He raised up and placed his mouth over hers, his tongue lightly exploring the barrier of her lips. He felt them tremble, then on a moan, Jamey surged into his kiss, unlocking her jaw, unlocking the incredible secrets within.

He'd never tasted such sweetness. She dug her fingers into his hair as she sank fully onto his chest. Not missing a beat, he brought his hands up to grasp her waist, easing the pressure on his ribs, though he would gladly have endured much more pain if he could go on kissing her, feeling her full breasts against his chest. Her long legs were hopelessly tangled with his, and he took pleasure in rediscovering their lovely leanness. As when they'd faced each other across his desk, he felt his body reorder its needs. Right now, he needed this woman.

Her initial hesitancy seemed to vanish as Jamey kissed him with abandon, and in the part of his mind that was still rational, he wondered at her being able to propel him to even greater heights of arousal with the relatively tame play of her lips and tongue and teeth with his. His response was almost instantaneous, like wildfire. The isolation here must have had more effect on him than he'd thought.

Either that, or she was one hell of a quick study.

He raised a hand to cradle the back of her head and found the thick braid at her nape. He wrapped his fingers around the rope of hair, liking the feel of firm silkiness against his palm, so like Jamey. He could grasp it tightly with the intensity of his pent-up desire without fear of hurting her. Yet Jamey was strong, as she'd told him, a physical complement to him. He yearned for completion, the physical bond that would seal the emotional one they'd established.

She kissed like she'd been born to it. A natural, which made the connection between them seem all the more true.

He'd almost think he was being seduced—except between the two of them, she was the less experienced. That great protectiveness he'd always felt where she was concerned encompassed them both as would the shade of an oak. And he realized what he would die to protect was not her, but them....

He tugged on her braid, dragging her mouth from his, intending to give them both a break, a return to sanity. She wriggled impatiently and tried to kiss him again. Kell bit back a groan. "Damn, Jamey, will you hold still?" he choked out.

She complied, resting her forehead against his as they both filled their lungs with much needed air. Yet she still seemed restless. Desperate. Also acting on instinct. That she might want him as involuntarily as he wanted her drove him wild. She'd braced one elbow next to his head, her other wrist bent as she ran eager fingers down the side of his neck, past his collarbone to tangle in the hair over his pectorals. The opening at her collar gaped, and Kell got a view of creamy white skin.

"Did you really think you could hide yourself under these baggy clothes?" he asked huskily.

"Didn't I?" she said. She seemed in a daze, her eyes smoky, her movements languid. Short nails lightly scratched his skin as she opened and closed her fingers almost as a cat would.

"No way," Kell rasped. This, in his mind, was not holding still, yet he was nearly helpless to stop her. Or himself.

Then she pressed her lips to the underside of his jaw, her tongue moistening the vulnerable skin. "I've been dyin' to do that," she muttered. And she did it again, this time scoring the spot with her teeth.

Kell's eyes shot open. He'd never considered that one of his erogenous zones but—

He caught her under the armpits, lifting her so they were nose to nose. "Damn*nation*," he part groaned, part gasped, part growled. "Where'd you learn *that*?"

He hadn't meant it literally, yet her head reared back, eyes wide with shock, as if he'd invaded her mind, discovered something about her she hadn't wanted known—or was ashamed of. Jamey sat back on her heels and stared at Kell as if she'd never seen him before. Then she covered her face with trembling hands.

"What am I *doing*?" Her tone was horrified. "What's wrong with me?"

Completely baffled by her reaction, Kell nevertheless sat up quickly, legs bent with her kneeling between them, and smoothed back her hair in reassurance. "Jamey, what do you mean? There's nothing wrong with you. We've done nothing wrong."

She looked up, appalled fear in her eyes. "What *is* it about cowboys? It's like I can't say no!"

"That's my fault, sweetheart. I overwhelmed you—"

"It's not you!" she interrupted, again taking him aback. "Didn't I learn anything?" Then she muttered miserably, "This is how it happened before."

"*What* happened?" he asked, not certain he wanted to know.

"With—" Realization struck her. Her gaze dropped to her hands twisting in her lap. Jamey said nothing, and he sensed her struggling within herself. Finally, head bent, she said, "I was—there was this cowboy. In the rodeo."

He dropped the hand stroking her hair. So he'd been right about her recognizing Clan, though it wasn't Clan she was talking about. She'd stated emphatically that she was not a buckle bunny, but it occurred to him now it was probably because she'd been hurt by the cowboy she just mentioned.

"Kell." She placed a tentative hand on his forearm propped on his knee. "Kell, the problem's not with you."

"That's pretty clear."

"I mean, it's me. I don't know my head from a bucket when it comes to cowboys."

"I see." All too well, in fact, because just today he'd proven he was *not* a cowboy, in both word and deed. His uncle had never debated the wisdom or feasibility of the course he chose—not out loud, at least, and Kell would bet Jamey's father never had, either. No, they'd been taciturn men, who they were and what they stood for was set in stone. No analysis necessary. No talking things through, especially not failures.

And now to learn that there was someone else, a *real* cowboy who rode the rodeo, whom Jamey had regarded so highly... had fallen in love with, from all appearances. A man apparently different from himself.

"I'm sorry, Jamey," Kell finally said.

She looked up at him. "Sorry?"

"Sorry to have—" he searched for the right expression "—led you on, I guess."

Again she shook her head violently. "No. It—it takes two to tango, I know that." She gave him a pleading look. "Kell, I'm tryin' to be honest with you. I've wanted to, from the start. But there are some things I just need to work out for myself first."

Kell wondered at the masochistic bent in him that made him ask, "Is it over between you and the cowboy?"

"Yes. No." She passed a hand over her forehead. "Sometimes I wish it was, that I could forget, or I wish— you know, that things had been different, but then...I can't. That's why, with you and me—I can't repeat my mistakes, Kell. I can't get involved with you. I just can't," she ended on an agonized whisper.

So. She did carry a torch for this rodeo buck. And whatever Kell's own appeal to her, it was probably something other than emotional. He felt like a fool even as inside him there set off a predatory urge to hunt down this faithless scoundrel and take him to task for the grief he'd caused

Jamey. Kell recognized his deliberation as a very cowboy-like need to attack a problem, make it a tangible force to be reckoned with, to be defeated. And if he'd been more of a cowboy—more like his friend Clan, for instance—he'd likely never question such an impulse. But Kell wasn't Clan. He *did* question the folly of tilting with windmills, romantic but futile oaths to break this land, master this weather...tame that Brahman...bring them all to heel by sheer strength of will. It struck him that this was the real reason he'd never be the kind of cowboy his uncle had been.

Or the kind of man he greatly suspected that Jamey would love.

He glanced up and saw the heartache written all over her face. Futile—because the cost to Jamey's self-confidence had already been exacted.

Kell touched the back of his fingers to her cheek. "It's okay, Jamey. What's done is done, right?" She nodded jerkily, clearly still upset. More than ever, he saw her as a vulnerable woman in need of protection. The difference now was that he didn't consider himself the man for the job.

"And we are who we are," he added, hoping to reassure her, make an explanation about himself.

Her gray-green eyes widened in understanding before she said sadly, "Yes. We are."

She slid off the bed as he thanked her for her doctoring. After she'd left, Kell sank back down on the bed as the aches he'd been holding at bay returned, worse than before. Because now an additional weight bore down on him beyond his failure that day as a cowboy.

Chapter Seven

Jamey paced the length of floor from one end of the kitchen to the other. Every fourth trip she paused at the door and peered outside, once again looking for Kell. This time, though, she worried about all of the boys who had yet to appear out of the March snowstorm raging its way across the Panhandle.

Midafternoon, yet the visibility was as at midnight. The wind drove the snow almost vertically against the side of the house. It was the kind of storm in which cattle suffocated, calves froze to death. And men lost their way home.

Jamey had made a big pot of coffee, hoping against hope it would be needed—and soon. She'd phoned her mother, three times, to ensure Glenna and Hettie were safe, warm, and stocked with plenty of diapers and formula. The radio continued to relate weather reports on the cold front that had taken the Panhandle by surprise. Jamey had news aplenty, but that was all she had. And it drove her crazy. She wasn't cut out for the role of ranch wife, waiting for her menfolk to return, helpless to aid them with anything but prayer. Pray Jamey did, however, for she had the added worry of having experienced the other side, that of trying to find direction in impossible conditions.

She didn't fool herself that she worried as much about the other men as she did about Kell. If he'd worked Plum Creek only in the summer, getting caught in a snowstorm was a new—and dangerous—experience for him.

How had her mother endured the worry all those years? Jamey guessed the only way was truly to have faith.

Wrapping her arms around herself as she stared into bright white nothingness, she regretted the awkwardness between them these past few weeks since Kell's run-in with the Hell Cow. And the official recognition of their attraction to each other. Kissing him had been like...like she had no control over her mind or body. She'd wanted Kell on the most basic of levels. She still didn't understand what in her had turned loose, but Kell was right: what's done was done, and she was who she was.

She couldn't rewrite the past, but she'd very nearly repeated it.

Even harder to quell than her physical response to him was the need to help him, to encourage him, to talk to him about the ranch and how things were going. She refused to give that up. It seemed he, too, was unable to sever that connection, and they'd gotten in the habit of talking over the day's events in the evening. But they kept a physical distance.

A dark shape appeared through the blizzard. It became more substantial with its approach to form a man on horseback. Donning coat, hat and gloves, Jamey flew to the back door and opened it.

She'd taken the precaution earlier of tying a rope to the porch rail, and she hurriedly looped the end around her waist. Snow pelted the length of her, stinging her face and nearly blinding her, yet she kept the form in sight as she plowed toward it, hoping and praying...

It was Kell. She said a brief thanks.

He saw her, too, and spurred Gringo forward. "Jamey! What're you doing out in this? Get back in the house!"

"I'm secured," she shouted back, reaching him and catching the gelding's bridle to hold both of them steady against the forceful wind. "Where're the boys?"

"I'm hoping they went to the Sheltons'. I figure they were closer to there than here when the storm hit, trying to head the cattle in the north sections toward the south fence." His hat was pulled down over his eyebrows, a scarf covered his nose and mouth. Both were crusted with snow. Worry radiated from him, too—worry for his men, his cattle, his ranch. A storm like this could mean death to any or all.

Her heart ached for him. He looked frozen clear through. "We need to get you inside where it's warm," Jamey said. It was the most either of them could do right now.

"Can't. I finally found the pregnant Hereford I'd been looking for—the one who followed the Hell Cow everywhere. She went off by herself, that's why she was so hard to find."

Some heifers were naturally easy calvers, yet all were watched the first time. "Has she had her calf?"

Kell looked grim. "No. But she's in labor."

From his tone, it sounded like they had a difficult delivery ahead of them. Depending on when she'd been bred, that could be the reason the heifer was calving late, after nearly every other calf had hit the ground. Or, if she'd been bred to a large bull... there was the possibility the unborn calf was too big to be born and had died in the heifer's womb.

"Going into labor is a good sign," Jamey shouted reassurance, as much for her own benefit as Kell's.

He nodded. "I stuck her in the maternity pen in the barn and came to get you." Only his eyes showed, but that was all she needed to see as he said, "I need your help, Jamey."

"Yes, you do." He'd probably pulled a few calves in his time, but it was hard work and often took two people. "I need to go back to the house and get a few things. You go settle Gringo, and I'll be along fast as I can."

Within ten minutes Jamey had reached the barn, where Kell had already joined the heifer in the pen. Restless, the animal lay down, then returned to her feet, then lay down again, over and over as she searched for a comfortable position she seemed never to find. Jamey could relate, her own birthing experience vivid in her mind. The cow lifted her white face and bellowed in pain and fear.

"That's right, Bessie," she said, naming the creature on the spot; she had to. "Let it all hang out, little momma."

Kell joined her once he'd seen to his horse. With difficulty, they maneuvered the heifer into a standing position against the side of the pen, where it needed to be if Jamey and Kell were to help her. Their breaths mingled as they both bent to get a better view of what was going on with the birth.

"There's a hoof showing," Jamey said. "Just one, though. One of us needs to go in and get the other leg squared away. You got the come-along?" Not waiting for his answer, she stripped off her jacket and shirt, under which she wore a pair of men's longies. Gooseflesh rose on her arms as she pushed up the sleeves and sluiced soapy water over her skin. It was cold in the barn, but she'd warm up quickly once the action started.

Then she caught Kell's assessing gaze, and she guessed it was because she'd just assumed the role of authority. Yet there was no question who knew more in this instance, and she wasn't going to back off just to soothe male sensibilities.

That didn't seem to be Kell's problem, though. Jamey glanced down at herself. She went braless most days she worked around the house, since her serviceable long underwear certainly covered her decently. Yet without her shirt, the fitted material showed in detail the full, feminine curves of her breasts.

Raising her head, she met his eyes. She didn't care if Kell saw her this way. This was her, Jamey Dunn. A woman. She had tired of hiding it.

Neither of them said a word as they stood in the freezing barn. Then Kell unbuttoned his own jacket and slid out of it. "I take it only one of us needs to examine the heifer."

"Yes."

"Then go ahead. Just let me know when you need me," he said, giving her the lead.

"Let's get the chains washed. Bessie, too, as best we can," Jamey instructed, all business. In normal circumstances out on the range, measures to prevent infection would have been irrelevant. Here, though, there was no reason not to take precautions. "Get a loop around the leg that's showing. Double the chain over," she advised Kell. "Less strain on the little one's ankle."

Using a calf puller required a gentle hand, much as an obstetrician needed in using forceps. Jamey secured the leg chain, all the while posed to jump out of the way should Bessie become agitated. Yet the heifer, while certainly not calm, seemed manageable. Gently, Jamey pushed the calf's leg back inside the heifer so she could grasp and pull forward the foreleg that was bent, then secure it with a leg chain, as well. Jamey hoped this was all that had been causing Bessie's difficulty. She made sure the calf's head was positioned between its legs, like it was ready to dive into the world. Then Jamey waited to see what kind of presentation Bessie could get with her own contractions. The next one came, producing little results. Minutes later, another contraction, but still no movement of the calf out of the birth canal.

"Should I put some traction on the chains?" Kell asked.

"A little. Not too much, though. Work with her contractions."

Kell obliged, giving the jacklike handle a pump to wind the chain around the ratchet and pull it tighter.

Yet after several contractions, little changed in Bessie's condition, except that the heifer seemed to be tiring. Jamey frowned. The calf was apparently too big for Bessie to birth. She was inclined to continue letting nature take its course, but there was always the danger of the umbilical cord getting pinched off or detaching. The calf would then try to breathe on its own. Any mucus or fluids in its nose and windpipe would be sucked into its lungs, drowning it.

At the thought, Jamey's own breath caught in her throat.

"That's not going to happen," she muttered fiercely.

"I could pull harder, the chain's not too tight," Kell said from behind her.

"All right, but let's not force it." She tried to call up her every experience pulling calves, tried to think as her father would have. If a choice had to be made, saving the cow took precedence over the calf. Pulling too hard with the chains could tear a cow up, injuring her for life. But Jamey was thinking like a woman right now. Like a mother. She thought of her own defenseless baby, how Hettie depended on her for everything in the infant's world. And how great that responsibility was. Suddenly, saving this baby, saving the mother, too, paralleled Jamey's own struggle to do her best for herself and her child.

"Jamey." At Kell's voice, she distractedly looked over her shoulder. His expression was determined. "We need to get this calf delivered. The contractions are growing less frequent and weaker. The calf isn't trying very hard to be born."

"It's going to be fine," she contradicted him, laying a protective hand on Bessie's rust-colored hindquarters. She wouldn't give up!

"Is it? Jamey, I've bowed to your expertise, but I've got my own instincts about these things, too. We need to get that calf out of there. Even now, I'm not sure it has a chance. And if it's already dead..."

"No!" She rounded on him, well aware of what he was suggesting. It was one of the most grisly parts of ranch life, having to surgically remove a calf from its mother's uterus. "Give Bessie time, work with her contractions."

"I have been. She's tiring, though. The calf's not budging." He paused as if searching for another tack. "Look, Bud always—"

"And my daddy did, too, just yanked away with the impatience of a man! Obviously none of you ever had a baby!" In a corner of her mind she registered the rise in her voice, the near hysteria in it. "You know, a lot of those old-timers believe in survival of the fittest, just letting the cow die out on the range with her calf half out of her, dead, too. If she's not a good breeder, why try to save her! Is that how you feel, Kell?"

She could see she'd startled him with her attack, but his answer mattered to her, very much.

"I don't ranch that way, Jamey," he said in steely tones.

"Then, please," she begged. "Give them both a chance!"

She turned away, not wanting to see if he agreed or not. There was no increased tension on the chains, however.

Yet the situation did not improve. Finally, Kell didn't ask for permission. He pumped the jack handle with slow and steady pressure as Jamey held on to Bessie and tried not to cry. It was like her own heart had dropped out of her as she heard the soft thud of the calf falling onto the padding of sawdust and straw. Immediately she bent next to the wet, limp form, deftly lifting it by its hind feet as if it didn't weigh as much as her. Kell reached her side and took the calf from her. He shook it, and Jamey dropped to her knees to clean out its throat and nose. There was no response. Drawing back her arm, she whacked the calf against its side with the flat of her hand.

Still, there was no movement, and Jamey died a little inside.

Kell eased the lifeless calf back onto the straw and stepped away. Jamey couldn't give up, though, not yet, as she shook it again. Shook it hard. Then Bessie turned and nosed her aside, sniffing her baby.

"No." Jamey pushed her back. "Don't. Don't get attached."

"Leave her alone, Jamey," Kell said, taking her shoulders from behind and pulling her to her feet. "Leave them both."

Jamey closed her eyes against the dull ache growing sharp within her breast. Her eyes stung, her throat felt thick. She couldn't cry. Anyone with experience wouldn't be so moved. Life and death—that's what ranching was all about. And survival.

She opened her eyes as the heifer raised her head, large brown eyes luminous in the fading light. She began to bawl for her dead calf.

Jamey turned her head and wiped her runny nose against her shoulder. She was shivering; God, she felt cold. As if he'd heard her thoughts, Kell draped her coat over her shoulders.

"Where's a bucket?" she asked, needing to take action, to do *something*. "Her bag's full of milk."

"It's best not to milk her, better to let her dry up—"

"We can't let the poor thing suffer!" Her voice cracked.

"All right, let me," Kell said, his hands on her upper arms turning her away. "You go back to the house and clean up. Let me take care of things here."

Wanting to take responsibility for the heifer, not wanting to abandon her, Jamey almost disagreed, yet if she stayed she knew she'd break down completely.

She fled to the house, to her room, shedding her clothes as soon as she stepped through the door. She dove into the shower, not waiting for the water to warm, though when it did she turned it up as hot as she could stand it, and still didn't feel it was enough to wash away her failure.

She'd failed, in so many ways. Failed Kell. He needed every calf, and with this snowstorm he was bound to lose at least a few.

She'd failed. Even if odds were the calf would have died anyway, Jamey bore the weight of its death harder than anything this past year. Yes, she'd held off making judgments of failures or mistakes in her life, yet this episode seemed a telling point. She had let her judgment be clouded by her feelings as a woman and mother, making her wonder if she really could be a good cowboy. Was she wishing on a star to want to be all three?

And what would she do if she was? Give up, again? Run on home to Momma, try to pretend today had never happened and she'd not failed—again?

The water beat down on her, yet it couldn't drive from her mind the images of the heifer and its dead baby. Her father, her mother, *her* baby.

We are who we are, Kell had said. Yet who was she? She knew who, or rather what, she wanted to be: a good mother, a good daughter, a good cowgirl. Who she was at present, though, that was harder to understand. She'd taken Kell's statement to mean she couldn't change the kind of person she was, and so should accept herself for her. If that were so, then all her efforts these past months were for naught, because her greatest fear was that she couldn't be loved for who she was—right now.

Jamey turned off the water as a sudden urgency overcame her. She dried off and dressed in jeans and a warm shirt, barely pausing to comb through her long, wet hair before making her way to the main house where the phone was. Normally she called her mother when she was assured of privacy, but Jamey couldn't wait. She had to talk to Hettie, had to find that connection with her daughter. Had to know that Hettie needed her as she needed no one else.

Entering the porch, she scuffed her boots across the mat. She listened for a moment, hearing nothing but the radio, which had returned to playing music. Yet on entering the kitchen she came up short when she spied Kell leaning against the counter, coffee cup in hand.

He'd obviously showered, too. Had obviously been waiting for her. He was the last person she wanted to see.

Jamey stood rooted to the floor, torn by the conflict inside her. She could see the phone sitting on its table down the hall. It'd become a lifeline of sorts for her, pulling her toward it and sanctuary. Yet this man stood between her and her refuge.

"Jamey," Kell said quietly.

"I need to make a phone call." The band of tightness around her chest grew a little tighter. "I— Can I use your office?"

He set his cup down. "Jamey, it wasn't your fault the calf died. I think it was a hopeless cause from the first."

She tried to brush past him. He caught her arm. "It wasn't your fault, sweetheart," he repeated. "You tried. Gave it your best."

Jamey jerked out of his grip. "If I had, it would have lived!" she flung at him. "Now just let *me* be!"

His eyes were worried and concerned as they gazed down into her defiant ones. "Dance with me, Jamey," he said abruptly.

"*What?*"

He tilted his head toward the radio. "Dance with me."

She stared at him, wondering who'd gone crazy, him or her. "You can't be serious."

"I am." He tugged her around in front of him, Jamey resisting all the way. But not very hard. Once he touched her, it was always so hard to resist.

"Why?" she whispered hoarsely.

"Because it's as good a reason as any to hold you for a while. Let me, Jamey," he said, his own voice dropping.

Gently, Kell pulled her against him, one hand spread on her spine, the other holding hers tucked against his shoulder. Her temple brushed against his rough jaw. Jamey tried, she really did, to hold herself stiff, separate, tried not to give in to the warmth and understanding surrounding her. But she felt herself thawing. Felt herself giving up. No—giving in.

The need to connect with her child—the child that logic reasserted was fine—was supplanted by the powerful connection that had always existed between her and this man.

They barely moved, more or less swayed in time to Garth Brooks's emotional rendition of "The Dance." His vibrant voice swirled around them as he sang of regrets, wonderings of whether a person would change their actions should they know beforehand how their life would play out. And the message came through that the pain was worth not missing the joys.

The two were inescapably linked—pain and joy—just like life and death. The incredible pain of her father dying, the wondrous joy of Hettie's birth. Looking back, what would she do differently if she had the chance? What might she have prevented? But what would she have lost as a result?

It was the wrong song for Jamey's state of mind. Again, she desperately swallowed back tears. In all the months of heartache she'd not cried in front of anyone, and keeping up that pretense, keeping that secret, was foremost in her mind. If the tears started here, with Kell, then it *would* be like giving up. She couldn't do that.

She clung to Kell, to his strength, and he clasped her to him oh, so tightly, so urgently. And she realized that he held her for his own comfort, too. To ease his own disappointments and failures.

"Kell," she choked, her nose nearly buried in his collar, "whatever happens with this storm, no matter if you lose more cattle than you think you can stand, please, don't give up Plum Creek. I—I've seen how discouraged you've been, and I want you to know, I'm here. I'll make up for tonight, I will—"

"Jamey, you don't have to do that. You can't, in fact."

"Then I'll help, do whatever I can do. Just don't give up."

He released her hand and lifted her chin. One thumb brushed at something on her cheek. It wasn't a tear, she told herself. "I told you, sweetheart, I won't. God help me, I can't."

She looked up to him, seeing for the first time the linking of opposites that formed the character in his face: strength and tenderness, discouragement and resolve, protectiveness and...trust. Jamey found regarding him almost too much to bear.

Lowering her chin, she muttered, completely off the subject, "I'm a terrible dancer."

"I'm not too swift myself." His mouth, of which she had a side view, curved upward. "Guess I should learn how to do the country swing, all those other smooth moves."

"You're doing fine," Jamey said, thinking of Henry and his *smooth moves*. "Some cowboys put as much into learnin' to dance as they do roping—Kell. I—I can't believe I said that," she stammered, mortified. "I didn't mean that you—"

"It's all right, Jamey."

"I just meant some men are more interested in bein' a cowgirl's sweetheart than doin' their jobs."

"You mean, cowboys," he murmured into her ear. "And I haven't been much of one." His voice wasn't bitter, just resigned.

"But I haven't been much of a cowgirl," she admitted, and again perceived her blunder. "Not that I want you...to be..." Her voice trailed off. He'd been the one to call her sweetheart twice this evening.

"Jamey," Kell said softly. "I've been watching you the past month. You've made real progress with Rosie. Kit told me how you know just what to do with the sick cows Purdy and Charley bring in. And I've appreciated your help and advice to me."

"But today, with the calf—"

"You gave your all, to the best of your knowledge. That calf just wasn't meant to live, and it's no one's fault."

"Yes, it is." Difficult as it was for her, she raised her chin to look at him, wanting as always to be as honest as she could with him. "I let my judgment be clouded. I was thinkin' like a mo—like a woman. I needed to think like a cowboy."

His lashes flickered as his gaze took in her face. "I'm not so sure. You may not have been able to save the calf, but you saved the cow. Like you said, a lot of ranchers would see the heifer as a liability now."

"And you? What's going to happen to Bessie, Kell?"

"She'll get another chance. This was her first pregnancy. We'll breed her to a smaller bull next time." He studied her thoughtfully. "Don't *you* believe she deserves another chance?"

"Yes," Jamey said fiercely. "Yes, I do."

"And I believe you deserve one, too. You've proven you can handle more than I was willing to give you credit for, and that you really care what happens to these animals. I'd be a fool not to take advantage of you," he said on a wry smile, wringing an abashed one from Jamey, despite herself. "I've thought about the job you want as a ranch hand, and I'd like you to have the official responsibility of taking care of the horses and cows in the corrals here at the ranch. Josh and Kit will be finished up with their work by roundup, and I need someone around the pens. You'll be busy, because you'll still be handling the housework and cooking, but I'll increase your wages, so hopefully it'll be worth it."

They'd abandoned any pretense of moving to the music as she stood in the circle of his arms. Jamey saw he was sincere, and felt a mixture of happiness and guilt and apprehension. It was what she'd been working toward, or close to it, and yet now she didn't feel deserving of Kell's faith in her. Especially since, sometime in the past few weeks, her goal had somehow changed from wanting herself to succeed to wanting more than life to see him succeed. And she had failed him!

"You just feel sorry for me," she said in faint denial.

"No. I don't know if this is the right thing to do, for either of us. But you do deserve a chance to prove yourself. Sometimes, Jamey," Kell went on slowly, "you almost make me believe that you could do whatever you set out to."

She pulled back and stared up at him. His gaze owned hers, told her he spoke with his heart. And at that moment Jamey fell thoroughly in love with Kell Hamilton.

Her hands rose to take his face between her palms, the tips of her fingers brushing the hair at his temples. Then she drew his head down and kissed him with all her might.

He hesitated for a split second before he tightened his arm around her and opened his mouth over hers. She gave it to him to do what he would with it. Which was to shift and slide, make the most of the moist contact between sensitive lips and tongues. The grazing touch of his mouth was almost too much, but the hard melding of it to hers was even more difficult to bear. She simply couldn't get enough, couldn't get close enough.

God, she tried, though. The friction of rough denim against rough denim as they pressed together nearly drove her wild. She loved letting her head fall back to accommodate the descent of masculine lips from above. She loved feeling smaller. Loved feeling feminine.

Jamey had always secretly feared she had no judgment, no control over both mind and body when it came to men. She wasn't sure she'd changed her mind about that, but right now she was glad not to have control. She was glad to be "that kind of woman," who could give herself over completely to a man and the emotion that coursed between them. It was all that mattered. He was all she wanted.

Yes, right now they were simply man and woman, free of the complications of roles and expectations and fears, caught up in a timeless dance, the twining of bodies, souls and hearts. The essence of their existence had been simplified down to the two of them, and yet they were nothing without the complement of one to the other. They were greater than the sum of two, because of what they could do together. Create together.

"Oh, Kell. What made you the kind of man you are?" Jamey murmured against Kell's lips. She'd told her mother that being fair and dependable were hardly reasons to fall for a man, and yet right now they ranked right up there with one other—that of the age-old quest to find the best mate for her, a good father for her children. "I mean, your parents must have done somethin' incredibly right in raising you."

At her comment he pulled back slightly. "To tell the truth, they didn't do much raising at all." Though he continued to hold her tightly, a little of the passion cooled between them.

Jamey could have kicked herself for inadvertently touching a sore spot. She was tempted to draw them both back into their love play, yet she couldn't ignore the expression of regret that had entered Kell's eyes, even though he tried to hide it.

"Do you want to tell me what happened?" she asked as she had the evening of his roping accident. Unable to prevent herself, Jamey smoothed her hand across his cheek and into his hair in a spontaneous gesture of comfort.

Kell shrugged. "Nothing earth-shattering. I just didn't have the kind of childhood I think you had."

"Things weren't perfect between me and my daddy. He was your typical cowboy. Independent, stubborn as a mule. Protective. He always said I could do whatever I wanted, but then he...."

This was the subject she'd avoided with her mother. And she wanted to talk to Kell about it—but not now. Now was for him. "I'd like to tell you the whole story someday, but I want to hear yours right now. Even if I didn't have the same kind of experience you had, I might understand. I want to understand."

He shrugged again, but this time Jamey sensed the gesture hid a little less behind it. "My mother and father divorced when I was seven. After that point, neither was around much, off living their adult lives. I was left on my own a lot."

Kell let go of her to drift to the window over the kitchen sink. He stood, gazing out of it, fingers thrust into the back pockets of his jeans. Jamey wondered what he saw in the white blankness that she couldn't. She wrapped her arms around her middle. The coldness that had enveloped her in the barn returned with foreboding.

"My uncle got me for the summers. He was the only real parent figure I ever knew, rough and uncultivated as he was. He made me feel I belonged somewhere. Even when I returned to Dallas for the school year, it helped to know he was here on Plum Creek. I always considered it my real home, and Bud knew what it meant to me. That's why he left it to me, even though I'd never ranched before."

He turned to face her with seeming reluctance. "Some days I feel I've got such a test ahead of me, trying to figure out what Bud would do in a situation. And I believe I'm making progress, learning more about what to do." He removed his fingers from his pockets, his arms dropping to his sides, his stance tall. Jamey got the impression he was making a difficult confession. "But I've finally realized I'll never be the cowboy Bud was—I either wasn't born with his talent for it, or I didn't grow up with the kinds of influences he had. I intend to honor his faith in me, but I have to ranch my own way. It's the only way I'll be able to be happy with myself and what I'm doing with my life."

That conviction was what she most respected about him. It was what he'd confirm of her own aims, although Jamey sensed a glitch here, an incongruity. Not in her perception of him, but in his perception of her.

"And your parents? Where are they now?" She wasn't sure she wanted to know, yet had to ask. "Your...mother?"

"Dad remarried and lives in Houston. I used to see Mom when she came through Dallas. She's pretty driven with her career."

"Which is?"

"Motivational speaking," Kell answered with a wry shake of his head. "How to get and keep your career on track, with no mention of family."

Jamey let her gaze rove the planes and hollows of his finely formed face as she pictured clearly the dark-haired boy he must have been, who believed himself a mistake, or at the very least, an afterthought. Her heart went out to that child before it sank within her at his next words. "I'll always love Mom and Dad because they're my parents, but that doesn't change the fact that they probably should never have been parents."

She registered his reaction of disappointment, which brought back that desperate feeling, for she saw what was coming.

She made a last-ditch effort to stop it, even so. "Sometimes, though, things happen. *Life* happens," she said. Now he needed to understand her. And she needed to be truthful. "You don't know, Kell—" She faltered. "About..."

Tell him now! her conscience admonished her. *Tell him about Henry and Hettie.*

But she couldn't.

For the second time that evening Jamey had to look away from him. Her breath seemed trapped in her chest, as she felt trapped again. Every way she turned lay an unresolvable obstacle: of trying to do her best for Hettie by aiming for a job that fulfilled her—but that took her away from her baby and left the child's own needs unfulfilled. Of trying to reconcile herself to disappointing her parents, her father in particular, with her mistakes—while trying to believe that Hettie and consequently Henry were not mistakes. *Was* she trying to rewrite the past, in which a girl could grow up knowing she was loved for being herself as she turned into a woman with a woman's dreams? And as a woman, believing she really, truly could be whatever she wanted in this world?

Or should she accept her past and its influences on her, as Kell had?

What did she want from Kell? What role did she want him to play in her jumbled-up world? What need did she want him to fulfill in her?

Right now, she needed, and needed badly, his continued regard of her. She wanted him to go on believing in her, that she could do whatever she set out to do. Yet in trying for the career she loved, which would restore her self-respect, she lost ground as a mother. He didn't seem to have a real animosity toward his parents; it was more a caution. Once bitten, twice shy, as she was with cowboys. But after what he'd just told her, she couldn't see Kell admiring her for leaving her child.

Jamey remembered the message in his eyes the night he'd first kissed her here in this kitchen. She couldn't have it both ways. Still she knew that giving up on her own needs couldn't be the best for Hettie.

"Kell, about tonight..." She pushed her damp hair away from her face before shoving her palms into her back pockets as she fell back on her training—that of laconic cowboy, allowing her the distance she so needed right now. "I can imagine what you think, me throwin' myself at you all the time, but it won't happen again. I want to thank you for your faith in me, after the c-calf—" Through sheer will, she controlled the sudden choking in her throat. "I'll do a good job with my new duties. You can count on it. I won't fail."

A moment ticked by in which the radio announcer ran through his upcoming play list before cutting to commercial. Kell's face was impassive, as if he sought distance, too, and she knew she'd hurt this fine, honorable man. He opened his mouth as if to say something more, and she waited in agony. Always, he moved her most with the expression of the words she herself could never seem to find. All it would take was one word to cause her to lose control and make her run to him. But he merely nodded before leaving the kitchen. Five seconds later she heard his office door close.

She had a clear line of sight to the phone in the hall, a clear line to call and talk to her baby. But Jamey needed something more right now. She needed Kell, and she couldn't have him. She couldn't have it both ways.

And she died a little bit more inside.

Chapter Eight

Kell heard the rapid, hollow thud of boot heels approaching his office. The door swung open, and Jamey stood poised on the threshold, a look of worried regret and guilty hope mingling on her face. He'd been expecting her.

"Come on in," he said. She closed the door behind her and strode to the desk. She'd come from outdoors, that beat-up hat still on her head and a sheen of perspiration on her face that gave it a healthy glow.

From outside came the muted shouts of men's voices as equipment was readied for tomorrow's roundup. The April rains had been good, and now in May the buffalo grass was lush and such a pretty green it had fairly transformed the barren landscape into a captivating spectacle of contrasts, with windy, sunny days bracketed by garnet sunrises and crimson sunsets. These were the best times in a cowman's life, when he rode through his herd admiring the new calf crop. Kell knew he'd been lucky; as far as could be determined he'd lost only a few cows or calves in the snowstorm. Though a full six weeks after that terrible event, the next few days would tell the real tale of how Plum Creek had fared. And whether it would be able to go on.

"I heard from Purdy," she said breathlessly. An air of excitement surrounded her. "About Clan. Is he...is he hurt bad?"

"Injured his hand, but not so much he won't be able to ride the bulls again, is what Reid told me." Kell pictured Reid's face as the older man related the incident to him. He hadn't needed to be told that Reid found his son's intent to pursue such a hazardous occupation foolhardy, if not downright crazy, especially in light of this injury.

He recalled his conversation with Clan a few months ago, how the younger man had seemed an embodiment of that cowboy need to contain his environment, not because it was a cowboy's job or a cowboy's challenge, but because, Kell now realized, there were so many, many things in this world out of one's control, that a man had no chance of conquering.

Kell's gaze flickered over the woman standing before him. A shaft of now familiar frustration shot through him. He understood fully, for the first time, the cowboy way.

"I'm sorry Clan got hurt," Jamey said with sincerity, drawing Kell from his thoughts. "Bull riding is a dangerous sport."

"I imagine he knew that from the get-go. Well, the matter is, he's out of the roundup."

"I know." The worry took precedence in her expression. "Kell, I was thinkin'..." Jamey began, shifting onto one leg. For some reason she'd gone back to wearing the snug clothes she'd first appeared in that day back in January, though he noticed she'd lost weight, which made her less curvy while emphasizing her long legs even more.

He wrenched his gaze from them. "I figured you would be."

Now the guilty hope she'd come in with led in her expression. "I was thinkin' you need someone to fill the space in your crew."

"I could use a good cowboy," he allowed.

"Not just a good cowboy, but someone who knows somethin' about your operation."

Kell leaned back in his chair, physically widening the distance that both he and Jamey had established between them emotionally in the weeks since spring had come upon them, and tried to give her comment some objective thought.

In these parts the ranchers neighbored, meaning they helped out with their neighbor's roundup, ensuring free, competent help for their own. The work took place over several weekends, as during the week one's own ranch still needed to be run. Mainly, though, it was because the work was the most exhausting and arduous of the year, and even the hardiest cowboy and rugged mount needed the days' rest in between. As a result, there was never an excess of good cowboys.

"That would be ideal," Kell said matter-of-factly, which was how he said most things these days. Maintaining that distance. "Although I'd settle for an experienced hand who'll last through two days of backbreaking work."

He saw her register his meaning. "But we're talking about the roundup startin' tomorrow. You need someone handy." She lifted her chin. "Like me."

This was what he'd been expecting. "Jamey—"

"I can do the job, Kell," she jumped in. "You said I deserved a chance to prove myself. Th-that you believed in me. That's still true, isn't it?"

The desperation he'd seen in her from the first suffused her features. He couldn't let it muddy his judgment. "Yes, it is," he assured her. "But you've got a job to do. Feeding hungry cowboys is no small responsibility, you know."

"But I thought of that. I wouldn't leave you in the lurch. I've been fixing as much food as I could beforehand."

"And who's going to do what can't be prepared in advance," Kell challenged, "serve up the food and clean up afterward, if you're doing a hand's work?"

"I figured my mother could fill in for me there."

He knew he'd played right into her hand. "Your mother. In Borger."

"Sure. I don't mean to brag, but my mother is one of the best ranch cooks you'll find."

"And isn't it convenient that I don't have to 'find' her?" Kell said, nettled as always by her maneuvering. He stood. "Sounds to me like you've had this worked out in your mind for a while now, to just step in when the opportunity came up."

Her cheeks turned pink, even as she met his gaze defiantly. "Well, and what if I have? It would take care of all your problems."

"Oh, I don't think it's quite that simple." Thumb and forefinger hooked in one side of his waistband, he studied her. "All right, suppose you tell me what you'd ride on the roundup? Clan's stallion?"

"I'd ride Rosie, of course."

"Of course." He'd wanted distance, and now he'd found it. Kell wasn't annoyed, he was angry. Angry with Jamey for again disregarding caution and practicality in her all-consuming need to make ranch hand. "Jamey, that horse has never spent one day out in a pasture with a herd of cows."

"I've trained her with the ones in the pens, though. You've seen her. She's quick and smart. And strong." She seemed desperate again, as if they weren't talking about the mare. He recalled her assertion about her own strength in this very room. "She's got the bloodlines. She can last out there, I know it."

"You don't know it," he flatly contradicted her. "And I don't know it. She may perform just fine under controlled conditions, but the fact remains, Rosie's untried and untested. We're talking about a hundred agitated cows milling and circling, looking for a chance to bolt. A skittish horse can't be trusted not to panic. I'd be a damned fool to put her out in a critical situation like a roundup.''

Jamey's wide mouth twisted in stubbornness. "What you're sayin' is, you'd be a damned fool to put me out there."

"You've got the right of it," he confirmed.

Kell faced her down, and she gave the look right back to him, starting a stirring in his gut—that male need to dominate, the need to conquer. No, the need to recognize their opposing energies and find in them their complements, as when they'd danced.

It had been six weeks since he'd held her, since he'd kissed her and experienced that elemental match-up. Six weeks since he'd fallen for a cowgirl—who couldn't resist cowboys.

He was a damned fool already.

Twice she'd withdrawn from him in the heat of the moment, and he had to conclude it was because he still missed that mark. Still lacked something in her eyes.

Kell had pondered again and again the error in judgment that had caused him to pour out his concerns to her, admit to struggling with being a rancher and a cowboy. He'd already guessed Jamey wasn't used to such openness in the men she'd known, who said little and never voiced doubts. At least not to a woman.

Yet he'd wanted her to know him as a man who *did* have doubts. He recalled the closeness they'd shared in those moments when she'd offered her understanding. And when she'd opened up to him. He didn't think any less of her for expressing the doubts and fears that chased her. But obviously she found such soul-searching uncommon—at least from a man—and upsetting.

In the weeks during which he'd had to ask himself what happened the night of the snowstorm, Kell almost wished he'd given in to impulse, the same one that had propelled him to defeat her in arm wrestling, that had made him catch her to him and kiss her the first time. Although he had seen how he'd startled her, he'd gotten the strongest sense that he could have taken her into his arms again, overcome her reservations and swept her away once more, almost against the rational thought of either of them. He could have drawn her back into the dance. It was part of the danger and allure, the inevitability and irresistibility of man versus woman. Yet might did not make him right.

How could he be the cowboy she wanted, when he hated being that kind of man?

Kell needed, for himself, to act honorably and fairly, and to take responsibility for those who depended on him. The only way he could be happy with himself was to try his best to fulfill that obligation.

Which made him say firmly, "You're not taking Rosie out on the roundup, Jamey."

She pounced on the unspoken implication. "So I'll be riding another horse?"

"No. I'm going to have my hands full making up for Clan's absence and overseeing the roundup, I can't look out for you."

"I don't need baby-sitting!" she argued.

She was breathing hard; he was breathing hard. And they weren't getting anywhere. Kell went for an appeal to reason. "Jamey, try to understand my side of it. I have the other men and the ranch to consider here. The roundup crew's got to function as a team, and if there's a weak link in there, it costs everybody. I won't put my employees and neighbors into unnecessary danger. And nothing can change the fact that you're as untried and untested as Rosie. Besides, we're talking about incredibly hard work here. As much as you've tried to minimize it, you're a woman and simply not as strong as a man."

He saw her mouth work in agitation. Her gray-green eyes were huge. Somehow, Kell managed to keep his expression impassive.

"What you're sayin' is, we are who we are, and I shouldn't try to be somethin' else," she said in that husky voice that had always been his downfall, causing him almost to give in.

He did find himself promising, "I tell you what. Once we're past the roundup, I'll put you out with the other cowboys for a trial period."

"But by then..." Her shoulders drooped, and when she brought her hand up to tug at the front her shirt in that old gesture of hers, he saw her fingers tremble. "Kell, please. Don't do me this way. It's not fair to tell me you believe in me and then put me in a nice safe pen where nothin' can harm me. If I'm going to grow, I've got to stretch my boundaries."

"I am trying to be fair, Jamey, to the best of my ability."

"Are you? Are you sure you aren't just bein' protective?" Her fist clenched over her heart. "'Cause that's sure what it seems like to me. You say you believe in me, but you don't trust me to know what I'm doing. I know it's natural to feel that way, like my daddy did, but it doesn't make it right." Then she said, her tone resigned, "Or maybe that's just like a cowboy."

Kell was momentarily struck dumb. Just like her daddy? She sounded as if it were an offense, when he knew she worshipped her father. And he, Kell Hamilton, was just like a *cowboy?* He almost laughed. It was the last thing he'd expected her to accuse him of being.

But he was glad she had, because matters started clearing up in his mind. He remembered the things she'd said over the past few months about her father: how he'd taught her everything—about horses and cattle. About being a cowboy. Without knowing all the details, Kell knew that Jamey felt she had let her father down. He saw the pains she took to downplay her femininity, and perhaps it was because she had never been encouraged to be a woman.

In a flash of reasoning Kell saw that he had a chance to prove himself with Jamey—and that it didn't have anything to do with his being a cowboy. It had to do with letting *her* be one... No, it had to do with just letting her be herself, loving her—for herself. And believing in that person.

Scratching his cheek, he wondered if he was completely off the mark, if he was projecting his own motivations and needs on to Jamey. He tried the acid test of asking himself what Bud would have done.

It didn't matter what Bud would have done! He'd already figured out he couldn't be the cowboy his uncle had been; Kell knew now he didn't want to be the man Bud had been, either, living much of his life in isolation, never knowing the fulfillment of sharing himself and his goals with a woman who could love him—for himself.

This was what Kell wanted. And, like a cowboy, he was determined to get it.

"Fine, then," he said. "You've got your chance. It's damned risky, but I guess any caution I might've come to the Panhandle with has been pounded, baked or buffeted out of me by the unmerciful weather here." He rubbed his jaw, considering. "I'll move Josh up to flank. You'll ride drag."

Jamey's face, which had lit like a light bulb at his first statement, dimmed faintly at his last. "Drag?"

"That's right. It's boring, it's dusty, and it's always the job given to low man on the totem pole. You want me to be fair, that's fair." He lifted his eyebrows at the rebellious look she threw him.

"Will I be working the calves with the rest of the boys?" she asked with an air of acquiescence.

"We're using crowders and squeeze chutes, so you won't have to bust them and drag them to the fire." He shrugged.

"You'll do your share. But you need to know right now that I'm the boss here. You'll do what I say without question. Got that?"

"Yessir," she answered in her husky voice. Her excitement had returned. And Kell saw in her eyes the regard he thought he'd lost.

He gave her a steely glance and a curt nod of dismissal to hide the misgivings that assailed him now that the adrenal rush had subsided. He hoped to God he was doing right by giving Jamey the length of rope she so wanted. He'd never forgive himself if he let her have more than she could handle, or if she got hurt. And he hoped he wasn't doing this just to elevate himself in her estimation, but because it was the right thing to do—and would prove to himself that he was correct in pursuing that course.

He guessed he'd just have to have faith in both of them.

The first day of the roundup dawned clear and breezy, perfect weather in which to work calves. Everyone was up at dawn, and anticipation permeated the air almost as perceptibly as the sage crushed beneath hoof and boot heel. Even the horses sensed this wasn't just another day on the range and pranced nervously as they were trailered for the drive to the first pasture. Ranch sounds drifted on the wind: the distinctive *chink, chink, chink* of a cowboy walking in spurs, the subtle swish of leather chaps, the creak of saddles. In the background, the cottonwood shading the house murmured incessantly, the breeze through its leaves sounding like water cascading over rocks and providing an element of calm.

Kell tempered his own excitement as he directed the action. Yet every so often his attention fell on Jamey as she inspected her equipment and horse like a soldier going to battle. She was all business, adjusting both cinch and breast strap on her stock saddle, checking the rest of her tack. He'd already watched her play out her catch rope, give it an expert twirl or two before recoiling it and hooking it over her saddle horn. It was the first time he'd seen her in full cowboy garb of spurs and chaps, and he had to admit she looked natural in them—and sexy as hell, sorry hat and all.

Kell poured himself a cup of coffee from the pot heating on an outdoor burner and knew he wasn't the only one watching her lead Rosie to the trailer, the leather strings of Jamey's chaps crossing the back of her long legs just below the seat of her jeans and emphasizing her shapely behind. One of the extra men almost walked into a fence post for trying to keep her in his line of sight. Charley and Purdy, even Josh and Kit, were beginning to bristle—not at a woman doing their job, but like protective older brothers. Kell knew the feeling. Or something rather like it. He'd resisted cautioning them on how to treat her, either to look out for her or not give her a hard time. Let the situation unfold of its own accord, he told himself. Let things happen as they might. Let her prove herself by herself.

For the hundredth time he wondered if he'd made a mistake.

He watched as Jamey walked over to her mother, who'd arrived last night. Kell couldn't shake the feeling he knew Glenna Dunn. It was probably her resemblance to her daughter. Kell had been surprised at Glenna's youth. He wondered what she'd been doing these past months and if she truly did depend on Jamey for her welfare. From what he'd seen, Glenna was capable; she didn't seem the type to tie her daughter to her for security. In fact, right now she made a shooing motion at Jamey, who *had* been hovering.

Dumping the dregs of his coffee onto the ground, Kell decided it was time to stop wondering about Jamey Dunn and her mother. He had a roundup to orchestrate.

By nine-thirty the herd in the north pasture had been surrounded, thrown together, and driven to the working pen at the edge of the section without incident. Reid had backed the pickup into the pen and unloaded the squeeze chute and other equipment used for vaccinating, castrating, dehorning and branding. Even with the chute holding the calf immobile, it was hard, dirty, sweaty work. The day was hotting up already. The flies were incessant.

Yet Kell couldn't help feel a surge of satisfaction at the smoothness of the operation. Each man knew what to do and did it without instruction. When the last calf had gone through the chute, he gave the crew a moment's rest to get a drink of water, take a dip of snuff or load a fresh wad of tobacco into a cheek. Jamey, he noticed, had soaked through the back of her shirt with her exertion. Her face was streaked with dust. She had blood on her boots and a big smile on her face as one of the boys handed her a cup of water. She was loving this.

And, Kell had to admit as the day progressed, she was doing a great job. More than once she and Rosie went off after runaways, putting on a cutting show to bring the rogue cows back to the herd. The mare *was* quick and smart, her size and speed an advantage in this capacity.

As was Jamey's. By midafternoon she'd pretty much taken over dehorning when it became evident that her smaller hands were more suited to the detail work the messy task required. He watched her when, after dehorning an older cow, her shirtfront was drenched by a squirt of blood. She'd once boasted she wasn't squeamish, and true to that assertion, Jamey didn't even flinch but asked for a surgical clamp, just like a surgeon, and expertly found the bleeder vein, clamped and pulled on it to seal it off.

"Girl, I seen that done by many a cowboy worth his spurs," said Purdy, who was doing the branding. "But never so flashy."

Jamey grinned shyly at the praise, and this time the surge of emotion that rose in Kell was pride. She was some kind of cowboy, her gender this time providing a distinct edge.

Yet along with the pride came concern. Being a good cowgirl was so important to Jamey, seemed to define herself in her own mind. He wondered if she realized that it was her unique set of skills and talents that made her good. Being a woman and bringing those instincts to the job were what made her valuable. She didn't need uncommon strength or endurance; she didn't need nor was she expected, to do it all, only to do her best.

Kell was glad to finally realize that, and he hoped she'd come to this understanding about herself. Because he wanted her to realize it about him, too.

"You is just the best girl," Jamey cooed as she broke off another piece of cottonseed cake. "You's the prettiest, smartest, quickest girl around, ain't you, now?"

Rosie nickered her agreement, her large eyes shining in the moonlight, before taking the proffered savory from Jamey's hand. Jamey crossed her arms on the top rail of the corral fence, her chin resting atop them as she regarded the mare. Today had been one of the best days of her life, she decided. She was achy and tired and happy—happy to be doing something she loved again. She'd missed it so, needed that confirmation so very much.

And things couldn't have gone better; she'd even overheard Reid Shelton complimenting Glenna on the blueberry pie—which Jamey had baked! Of course, she thought with a private smile, Reid might have had an ulterior motive for sweet-talking her mother.

Glenna had handled the cooking admirably, as Jamey'd had no doubt she would. And she appreciated her mother stepping in, even though that had been the plan from the beginning.

Yes, everything was working out as planned. Since getting her ankle cast off, Glenna helped at the church preschool, and the minister's wife had been more than willing to return the favor by caring for Hettie for the weekend, since it would have been difficult to look after the baby with the constant activity of preparing and laying out the meals, helping serve them, and cleaning up afterward. Both women agreed it was better this way, and hopefully the last time Jamey and Hettie would have to be parted. Besides, Jamey had wanted one more chance to establish her competence as a cowboy in Kell's eyes so that he would see that motherhood, just like womanhood, was not a detriment to her getting the job done. She trusted Kell's sense of fairness not to hold her back from taking on even more ranch duties on those grounds alone.

But what of his personal feelings for her? On that thought, the jaws on the trap she'd felt caught in from the first seemed to clamp down even harder. She so wanted, so needed, his regard. But if his childhood had as much of an effect on him as hers had had on her, he might see her as having neglected her responsibility to her child. And would he be wrong? she asked herself, yet again. Jamey had wrestled with this guilt for months now. Today had confirmed her belief that she was right to pursue her calling. In the long run it would be better for Hettie, because she knew she'd teach her daughter by example, if no other way: she could be anything she wanted.

Although she'd not been exposed to much of the world outside her own concerns, Jamey knew she was not the only mother who struggled with the dilemma of trying to wear more than one hat at the same time. Many women raised their children without help, and it often wasn't a question of getting the job they were best at, or that fulfilled their own needs, but of getting any job at all. And Jamey knew that she was lucky. She clasped her hands, her forearms still resting on the rail, and sent out her hope and love to those women that they find a way to persevere.

She turned as she heard footsteps behind her. A tall form approached, one she recognized as Kell's. Her heart thumped in response. She'd hoped to have a minute alone with him, had yearned for it even as she'd dreaded it. And now her opportunity had come to put things to rights. He'd been honorable and fair with her; he deserved nothing less in return. She had to keep that at the front of her mind.

"How's Rosie holding up?" he asked, stopping next to the fence and giving the mare a pat on the neck. "It's going to be a long day tomorrow, too."

"She's fine," Jamey answered, pushing back a lock of hair, still damp from her shower. "She didn't have quite the workload as the mounts being ridden by the other cowboys."

"And you?" He leaned one hip against a fence post, facing her. "How are you holding up?"

"Fine, too." Avoiding Kell's eyes, she fed Rosie the last of the cottonseed cake. The warmth of his closeness was darned distracting. She remembered, vividly, how it felt to be held in those strong arms, how he'd kissed her with barely contained urgency with the mouth now turned down in thought. Yet most of all, she remembered his words of hope and faith and love: his hopes for himself—and for her—to be the kind of people they both so wanted to be; his faith that somehow he'd make a go of ranching in this hostile environment; and his love for those he respected, like his uncle. The cowboy.

She prayed she wasn't wrong about this cowboy.

"I thought everything went pretty well today, didn't you?" she said, wanting to reinforce her performance.

"It sure did. I thought *you* did pretty well."

Happiness unfolded in her even as the confession to come clean loomed like a storm cloud on the horizon. "I'd hoped you'd think so. I did my best. I—I wanted you to be proud of me," she blurted out rather desperately.

His hand covered hers as it rested on the fence rail. "I am, Jamey. Very proud."

That touch calmed her, as if she were a skittish horse in need of a firm hand. She threw him a fleeting smile. "You looked pretty sharp out there yourself," she said shyly. On his shrug, she asserted, "I mean it. The whole operation went like clockwork, and I know drivin' cattle is no cakewalk. If things went smoothly, it was because you know what you're doin'."

"Mmm." His chin dropped as he drew a pattern in the dirt with the toe of his boot. "I've got to admit, Jamey," he said slowly, "over the past few months I've felt like I was flying by the seat of my pants."

"But your instincts are right, and you don't let a bunch of male pride or cowboy arrogance muddle your thinkin'."

He gave a low chuckle. "I'll take that as a compliment. What I'm trying to say, though, is, thanks for your input these past months. It's helped a lot."

"I was glad to help, Kell." She turned to face him fully. "But the truth is, it wasn't my doing that got this ranch up and runnin' again. You've always done your best, too. The men trust you and look up to you because of that."

His face was expressionless, giving away nothing, yet Jamey knew as surely as if it were written on a page in front of her that, though he'd never wavered from his purpose, Kell had his own deep concerns at being able to live up to or handle the role he'd set himself into. In his mind, he had a mighty tall saddle to fill in his uncle's wake. And he'd filled it, sure, but in a whole different way than Bud Hamilton did. Kell had even said himself that he would never be the kind of rancher his uncle had been, and that was okay. Fitting, in fact.

In that moment, Jamey overlaid her own situation on that logic: she wasn't James Dunn; she wasn't Glenna, either. She wasn't the kind of cowboy her father had been, nor the kind of parent that either of them had been. She had learned from her mistakes; she could learn from theirs.

And Jamey found a measure of the peace that had eluded her for almost a year. She *was* a good mother, a good cowgirl, a good daughter—because she was doing the best she could.

She looked up at Kell, wanting to give him the confirmation he'd indirectly given her, just by being the kind of man he was. "You might've had some doubts about yourself when you took on Plum Creek," she said, her voice husky, this time because her heart was in her throat. "But now... you're some kind of cowboy, Kell Hamilton."

Those brown eyes of his glowed. Burned. "So are you, Jamey Dunn," he murmured. "So are you."

The indistinct light lent his features depth and texture, as it had the evening he'd stood battered and aching in the hallway. He was a fine figure of a man. His hair glistened, and she guessed he'd just come from a shower, too. For some reason, knowing he had made her weak inside.

They stood a foot apart, staring at each other. Then, as if choreographed, they moved into each other's arms.

His mouth was hot and open on contact, and Jamey moaned into it as she met the velvet play of his tongue with hers. He'd once said he needed this intimate touching with her; well, she needed it, too. Everything he could give her.

He was all cowboy, no argument there; and right now he made her feel nothing but all woman.

Down her spine slid one palm, and he thrust it into the back pocket of her snug jeans. His fingers curled slightly within that confinement while he set his other hand on her waist, bringing her more firmly against him. Jamey gasped and locked her arms around his hard torso, hooking her thumbs into his belt loops as if hanging on for the ride of her life.

And he did rock them as they went on kissing, a languid pitch and sway of legs shifting from hip to hip, a slow and sexy dance that took the breath right out of her.

Finally he lifted his head an inch, letting her take in the air he'd stolen from her. Jamey laid her cheek against Kell's shoulder, her forehead touching his jaw. She liked how they fit together. All it would take was a little from him, a little from her, and together they could make this feeling into something real and lasting. She knew it in her bones.

Now, her heart whispered. Now was the time. She needed to be honest and honorable with Kell; she needed to count on him being the same. And fair.

She needed to tell him about Hettie. But she didn't know how she'd bear his disappointment if it came.

"Kell, there's something I need to tell you."

"I know."

Her stomach leapt up in her like a deer out of the brush. "You know?"

He pulled back slightly and looked down at her. "You want to tell me about that raggedy-assed hat you wear like it's a precious crown. It was your father's, wasn't it?"

"Yes," she said softly, understanding. She gazed up at Kell. "I've pretty much set him up as some kind of king, haven't I?" She smoothed her fingers back across his roughened cheek. "He wasn't, though. He was just a man tryin' to do his best."

"I figured that."

"Oh, Kell, there's so much to tell you. More than just about Daddy—"

She was interrupted by the sound of a vehicle coming up the drive. A vehicle in bad need of a valve adjustment, its ticking one she recognized, even after all these months. Jamey stiffened in Kell's arms.

Twenty feet away a battered, dual-wheel pickup came to a stop under the illumination from the high yard light. The door opened and out sprang a whipcord-thin man as if from a rodeo chute. He slammed the door behind him and took a look around, adjusting the set of his cowboy hat and hitching up jeans so tight the gesture couldn't have been for anything but effect.

"Can I help you?" Kell asked, letting go of Jamey to step forward. She put out a hand to stop him—no, to stop time—and met nothing but air.

At the greeting, the man turned. The light caught the flash of a belt buckle large and shiny enough to signal a freight train at midnight. He started toward Kell and Jamey. "Well, now, the question is, can I help *you?* I'd stopped down the road back there to see how my buddy Clan Shelton was doin' after that wreck he got into, and he said y'all might be able to use a good cowboy for a few days."

"I might." Kell had reached the man, though Jamey still stood rooted to the spot next to the fence. She wanted to run, far as she could. "I'm the owner here. Kell Hamilton."

"Pleased to meet ya. Name's McSween."

Jamey made an involuntary sound, no more than a squeak, but the cowboy's eyes homed in on her like the man had a sixth sense for things such as locating the nearest female in ten miles.

He broke into a grin nearly as bright as his belt buckle. Smack dab in the front of his mouth shone a gold tooth. When had he acquired that? Jamey wondered.

"I'll be damned," he said. "Is that who I think it is?"

Kell turned, and she caught his look of puzzlement. Her heart sank. Oh, why hadn't she been given the chance to explain?

But she had, many times. And now it was too late.

"Henry," Jamey said weakly.

Kell frowned as he glanced from one to the other. "You two know each other?"

"'Pends on what you mean by 'knowing,'" Henry said suggestively. Now he glanced from Jamey to Kell as he marked the situation. "Din't she tell you, Hoss? Jamey here's my ex."

"Your ex *what?*" asked Kell.

Henry roared his laughter, throwing back his head with the abandon—or more accurately, the carelessness—with which he did everything. Clearly, he was delighted with the development of events. "Not my ex-what," he corrected, the gold tooth sparkling. "My ex-*wife!*"

Chapter Nine

"You've got to tell him," Glenna said before taking a sip of ice tea from the sweating glass she held.

"Tell Henry about Hettie, or Kell about them both?" Jamey asked on a tired sigh. The heat made her tired, sure. It was a real scorcher again, the second day of the roundup. And the hard work took its toll. But that wasn't what made her feel so bone-weary right now.

She set her empty plate on the grass and leaned back against the trunk of the cottonwood in the ranch yard. She'd tried all morning to get a moment alone with Kell to explain, but it had been impossible with the roundup going on. Last night he'd left almost immediately after Henry arrived, to find the cowboy a place to bunk and a horse for the next day. And, Jamey had an inkling, to avoid having to listen to her ex-husband greet her after nearly a year's separation. Yet she'd had nothing to say to Henry—then. Jamey had lain awake half the night trying to figure out what to do. Finally she'd decided to talk it over with her mother.

A burst of laughter came from the group of men gathered at one of the trestle tables set outside for lunch. The obvious center of attention was Henry. Kell was nowhere in sight, though when she'd sneaked into the house earlier to phone the baby-sitter and check on Hettie, the office door had been closed.

Henry looked like a regular dandy today in fancy, fringed, buckskin chaps. Another prize buckle drew attention to itself as sunshine glinted off it. So did the pair of engraved spurs he wore, their rowels like silver stars on his heels. He stood out from the other cowboys in their worn and dusty clothes, much more realistic for the work they were doing. But such impractical peacockery was as much a part of Henry as his name. In fact, when he glanced toward her and caught her looking at him, he shot her a satisfied smile, which Jamey, unimpressed, did not return. Surely he didn't think she'd fall for that song and dance again.

Glenna's gaze followed her daughter's. "Well, you've got to tell Henry, now that he's here. I'd hate to see you have to try to track him down at some other time with a child in tow."

"Yes, Henry needs to meet his daughter." Jamey stretched her legs out, crossing them at the ankle, and sighed again. "I don't know why, Momma, but tellin' him about Hettie scares the life out of me."

"Because you think he'll try to take Hettie away from you?"

"No. I was afraid at first, right after Hettie was born, that he might, but I think that was me goin' off the deep end with all that had happened. I wanted nothing more than to just keep Hettie to myself. I wanted her to be all mine." She swatted at a pesky fly. "Now, though...I know she isn't, in more ways than one. The minute I gave birth to her, she'd stopped bein' all mine."

"I think every mother feels that way," Glenna said softly.

Jamey nodded. "It's instinct kickin' in. Instinct I never thought I had till Hettie came along. But just because somethin's natural doesn't make it right." She lifted one shoulder. "Henry's her father, Momma. I can't hold up his being a lousy husband as reason not to give him his rightful chance to be a daddy to Hettie. I wasn't much of a wife, but hopefully I'm a good mother. Maybe he's got it in him to be a good parent, too."

"Maybe," Glenna agreed, though not very strongly. "Then why are you scared of tellin' him?"

"Like I said, I don't know. I just know I am."

Glenna set her own plate aside and wrapped her arms around her jeaned knees. "Maybe you're afraid of what Kell will think."

"That sure makes sense, doesn't it?" Jamey experienced another prick to her conscience, much like the ones that had been needling her since Henry had shown up. She wondered how Kell felt about this development. Hurt, for sure. Jealous? Quite possibly. Disappointed—definitely. With her, though it was no one's business but her own that she'd been married and divorced. However, it was Kell's business, his personal business, that she had a child, because the feelings between the two of them were personal. She'd had justification for keeping Hettie's existence from him as long as he was only her employer. But things had gotten all complicated when she fell in love with Kell. The possibility that he might see her as a neglectful mother had held her back from confiding in him. With Henry's arrival, she wondered if she'd already damaged Kell's regard for her beyond repair by making her appear to have been dishonest with him. Telling him about Hettie now just might be the end for any chance she had with Kell, but she couldn't put off telling him the truth indefinitely.

"I told you what he said about his parents and how they just about deserted him," she said to Glenna.

"But you said he found a sense of home and family at Plum Creek with his uncle."

"Yes. And he turned out a fine man. But I think that had more to do with Kell himself than his uncle." Jamey leaned forward to pick cockleburs off her jeans. "You know, I never understood much about men and how their minds work, and I think it's because I never knew a man who'd talk about such things. Daddy never did. Oh, he'd spend hours showin' me how to braid a rope or treat ailing cows. When I was little, I thought he knew everything about everything, and I suppose that's what he wanted me to think." She paused. "I—I know what he wanted me to think about myself—that I could do anything I wanted to. But he didn't seem to believe it."

"He did believe, sugar, or he wouldn't have planted that desire in your heart. I believe in it, too. But we both made a mistake. He wanted to hold you back, to keep you safe, and I let him try to." She brushed a straggle of perspiration-stiffened hair back from her daughter's face. "He didn't do it because he lacked faith in you. He was just following his natural instinct to protect his little girl."

Jamey nodded, soothed by her mother's touch. These were the words they'd both been avoiding for so long. Somehow it wasn't as difficult as Jamey had thought it would be to say them, and she guessed it was because she'd reached a different place in her thinking, in her feelings about herself.

"That's why I left a year ago," she said. "I know that now. I never thought I was the kind to rebel, and I don't guess that's what I was really doin'. But it wasn't fair of him not to send me off with his prayers," she stated without anger, "to hope he'd raised me right, have faith that what he'd taught me would see me through whatever I'd be up against in the world out there. And whatever mistakes I'd make."

She met her mother's loving gaze. "I don't regret what happened, Momma—Henry or Hettie. It wasn't my fault Daddy got sick and died, and we lost the ranch. I know that now. That's how life goes sometimes, and what's done is done. But I do regret that I never got the chance to mend things with him. To show him that I was going to make it on my own."

Glenna smiled gently. "No, you didn't, and that wasn't fair to either of you, was it? I do know his last thoughts were of you and your welfare. He loved you, no matter what had happened."

Jamey dropped her chin as her throat grew tight and her eyes began to sting. "I'm sorry, Momma," she whispered, saying the words she'd been wanting to for a year, even if she couldn't change the past.

"I'm sorry, too, Jamey, for not taking more of a hand with you, being more of a mother and providing a balance to your daddy's influence."

She wiped her eyes with the back of her hand and hoped none of the guys had eyesight good enough to see her distress. "What do you mean?"

"I guess I've always been the kind to sit back and hope things would work themselves out."

"Oh, but I've appreciated that, Momma. Most of the time," she added with the flash of an ironic smile, which Glenna returned.

Her heart full to bursting, Jamey groped for her mother's hand and found it. "You were always there for me if I needed you. And I always thought you were a good mother and wife."

"Thank you for that, sugar, but a lot of times I haven't thought so myself. All I can say is both your father and I loved you with all our hearts, and we did the best by you we knew how."

The tightness in Jamey's throat became almost suffocating, yet she swallowed it back and said, her voice cracking, "That's what I'm tryin' to do, too. The best I can. But what if Kell doesn't see it that way? What if he thinks I'm neglecting my baby?"

"Then he doesn't know you at all. You may think you've hidden your real self from him, but who you are is right out there as plain as the nose on your face for whoever wants to take a good look." Glenna put an arm around Jamey's shoulders and, not mother to daughter but woman to

woman, told her, "I see in you so many good things. A little of your daddy, a little of me. The best of us, I think. But
there's a lot that's just you. You're a special person unto
yourself, Jamey Dunn."

Jamey met Glenna's gaze. And what she saw there made
her believe that her mother loved her as a person, and would
love her, even if Jamey were not her daughter. She turned
toward Glenna and wrapped her arm around her mother's
neck, returning the hug. Then she pulled away and looked
at Glenna, not as her mother but as a woman, and thought
Glenna combined a unique blend of youth and maturity.
Jamey saw herself in twenty years, with lots of her life still
ahead of her. And with the experience behind her to make
those years her best.

"Thanks for all your help this past year," she said. "For
putting up with me while I worked things out."

"I was glad to be there for you. I'm still here for you.
You're going to need someone to take care of Hettie while
you work, and I've grown rather fond of my granddaughter."

"But you've got your own life to live now." Jamey's gaze
strayed to the group of men and picked out one in particular: the distinguished-looking Reid Shelton. "We'll see what
works out."

She let go a huge sigh of relief. "Whew! Things sure don't
seem so bad once you get them out in the open, do they?"

"Wiser words were never spoken," Glenna concurred.
Jamey knew what she meant.

She squared her shoulders. "Well, this afternoon we finish up for the weekend. I heard one of the hands sayin' everyone was going to get together for a little pickin' and
grinnin' tonight, since the neighbors helping out will be
leavin' right after the last of the calves has been worked.
That means Henry'll be leaving, too." She gave Glenna a
smile of love and hope and faith. Jamey would need them
all in the next hours. "I'll ask for your help one more time,
Momma."

"You got it, sugar."

"Here's what I need you to do...."

Kell lifted his hat and let the hot breeze dry the wet ring around his head left by his sweatband. And sweat he had, clear through to the outside of his straw Resistol. It, as well as his felt Stetson, had been new just a few months ago. Now it was stained and dusty and sun-baked and properly broken in. No one could look at either his hat or boots and mistake him for a weekend cowboy. A lot of good it did him, he thought cynically.

He sat on horseback and watched the crew bring in another bunch of cows and calves to be worked. With Henry McSween in the lineup, Kell had backed off and concentrated on directing the roundup. Except McSween didn't seem as easy in the saddle as Kell would have believed an experienced cowboy would be. It was nothing obvious, just a...feeling that this guy wasn't quite the wrangler he styled himself to be.

Or maybe it was just sour grapes on Kell's part.

Jamey's ex-husband. It was one thing to believe she'd had a romance with a man. Kell had had his share of relationships, too, and he wasn't one to apply the double standard. But for her to have married McSween, believing him to be some kind of cowboy when for all appearances he wasn't.... Kell knew Jamey had a discerning eye when it came to such matters, so he had to conclude McSween must have had another kind of allure, which Kell had yet to figure out. The guy was a braggart and a show-off and slick as they came. But he sure talked a good game. That must be what Jamey had seen in him.

The conclusion didn't set well with Kell. Not at all.

Kell squinted against the bright sun, surprised to see McSween at the front of the herd. Where was the regular crew? Yet the young cowboy was bringing the cattle in pretty as you please.

Then Kell saw that the Brahman led the herd, her four-month-old calf at her side. He could almost see the instant the cow realized they were headed toward the catch pen. Abruptly she veered to the left at a forty-five degree angle, taking the rest of the herd with her.

McSween spurred his sorrel to head the Brahman off, slapping his coiled rope against the thigh of his chaps and whistling through his teeth to get her to swerve toward the corral. Wrong move. This frightened the other cows, who turned back in the right direction, but now at a full-out run.

Kell assessed the situation in a split second. Someone—cowboy, horse or calf—was going to get trampled.

The other cowboys did their best both to keep the herd on course and slow it down. The Hell Cow, however, kept going left with the determination of a steamship heading out to sea, the obstacles in her way be damned. Her calf was like a little tugboat at her side. Kell himself was on a gallop toward what had the makings of a world-class wreck.

"Let her go!" he yelled to McSween. "We'll catch up with her later!" But by then McSween was chasing after the Brahman and her calf, hooting and hollering like a banshee, which only made the two animals speed up. Kell could see what he intended to do. McSween took up his rope and dropped a loop over the calf's head. The little one came off his feet and flipped over its end. Kell winced even as his anger doubled. He'd almost reached McSween when the young cowboy leapt from his saddle, in true rodeo style, and ran the length of his rope to the calf, which had regained its footing. He threw it to the ground again and tied up three of its legs. Like he was in some damned-fire rodeo.

McSween straightened, a pleased grin on his face, as Kell pulled up beside him. "You witless fool!" he said. "You wanna break its neck?"

McSween's smile dimmed. "I caught him, didn't I?"

"The object here is not to beat the clock but bring these animals in healthy. I can't sell an injured calf."

"Well, I—"

Both Kell and McSween caught sight of the Brahman, not twenty yards away. She was standing with her front legs braced, her head up, and as wild a look in her eye as Kell had ever seen. Angrily looping her tail, she charged McSween.

"Move!" Kell shouted. McSween leapt into his saddle, but he couldn't go far; the incapacitated calf was still tied to one end of his rope. And the home end was tied fast to his saddle horn.

Now it was a matter of saving cowboy and horse from injury, though Kell was tempted to let Henry get a good sample of the Hell Cow's fury. Yet he grabbed his own rope, even if he wasn't certain what he could do to prevent the Brahman from making contact. If he looped the cow in an effort to stop or slow her progress, he couldn't tie off or she might drag him and his horse down. Dallying his rope around his saddle horn would slow her for sure, but the rope would eventually play itself out and she'd reach McSween, anyway.

Then from the back of the herd came Jamey, riding like a wild Indian, her red braid bouncing on her back in a fiery tail. "You head her!" she called, dropping her reins. "I'll heel her!"

Jamey's appearance had caused the cow to redirect herself toward another target, and it was some intimidating sight to see half a ton of mother cow bearing down on him. Kell set himself, though, gave his rope an aiming twirl, and dropped it over the Brahman's head. She kept coming. But before she could go much farther, he saw Jamey actually stand up in the stirrups and swing a circle over her head, then let it fly. It caught the Brahman neatly by one hind leg. In a swift synchronization of movement, Jamey set herself into her saddle, dallied her rope and brought Rosie to a firm halt. The cow went down.

Between them, they held their ropes taut to keep the Brahman immobilized. Kell's gaze collided with Jamey's, and they both grinned spontaneously, somewhat from relief, but mostly, at least on Kell's part, from the accomplishment. *They* had performed in perfect synchronization, as if they'd practiced team roping a cow hundreds of times before.

The other cowboys had done their jobs of containing the stampeding cattle, and a few of them rode up now. Kell tossed the home end of his rope to Purdy and gestured for Jamey to do the same to Charley. "Ship 'em both. I can't afford to have a loco cow or her offspring in with my cattle. Why my uncle kept her, I don't know, but I haven't found enough reason to, no matter how good a breeder she is."

He glanced at Jamey for her reaction, half expecting her to make a case for the mother who was only protecting her baby. He knew how she felt about such things.

But she wasn't looking at either Kell or the Brahman. She was looking at McSween pensively.

Which reminded Kell that he had another matter to settle. He rode Gringo over to McSween, who'd dismounted once the danger was over and now stood by himself trying to punch the dent out of his stomped-on hat.

"You're outta here, McSween," Kell said from horseback. It briefly crossed his mind how this might seem a jealous retaliation to Jamey, but the fact was McSween had acted carelessly and recklessly, and no one put Kell's men or his cattle into that kind of unneeded danger. McSween might know how to rope as good as any other rodeo bum, but that didn't make him a cowboy. "You can walk your way back or talk your way back, I don't care. Just get your gear and leave."

"Wait!" Jamey rode forward, moving Rosie alongside Gringo. "He can't leave . . . not yet."

Everyone, including McSween, stared at her in disbelief. But she was looking at Kell, her eyes pleading with him. For a fleeting moment he wondered if he'd unknowingly slipped into some alternate universe where everything was reversed, because this made absolutely no sense at all. Why did she want McSween to stay? Kell could tell that none of

the men, even McSween himself, found Kell's order anything but justifiable. His word as ranch boss was unques-
tionable.

Belatedly, Jamey seemed to realize this. "I mean, can't he
wait to go?" Her voice dropped to a whisper meant only for
his ears. "Please, Kell, I wouldn't ask if it wasn't important."

Did she really want him to back down in front of his men
and let McSween stay? What *was* it about this cowboy? Or
was there some little-known cowboy convention he wasn't
aware of that would justify giving this negligent S.O.B. another chance?

Why couldn't Jamey see the kind of man McSween was?
Kell wanted to shake some sense into her, like a foolish
schoolgirl in need of a talking to. But he wasn't her father.
He had no claim on her except as her employer. And she'd
proven she knew what she was doing in her job. He'd have
been in a real bind with the Brahman if it hadn't been for her
help. So did she know what she was doing now?

He glanced across the circle of cowboys and met the eyes
of McSween, arms crossed over his chest and a smirk on his
face. And Kell knew it wasn't a matter of cowboy pride or
masculine domination. This guy was trouble and Kell would
be a fool to put him into another risky situation.

He jabbed his thumb over one shoulder like an umpire
calling an out. "McSween goes. I don't want to see him on
my property again."

No one said a discernible word, though there were mur-
murs and nods as the crew returned to work, leaving Jamey,
McSween and Kell in a triangle. Cocky to the last, Mc-
Sween gave a bow and said, "It's been a pleasure helpin' you
out with your first roundup, Hoss." His implication was
clear. Good grief, this guy had the ego of King Kong! Was
that what Jamey saw in him?

Kell said nothing, revealed nothing.

McSween turned to Jamey, her face a mask of preoccupation as she gazed down at him. That didn't stop him slid-

ing his hand under her chaps to grasp her ankle. "Jamey, darlin', if I'da known you still cared—"

"Don't, Henry," she said hoarsely.

McSween dropped his hand with a shrug. Then he uncinched his saddle, swung it over his shoulder, and ambled off with all the aplomb of the Duke riding into the sunset.

Jamey watched him go—like he *was* John Wayne. Like she wanted to go after him, and Kell's disappointment in her ran neck-and-neck with the discouragement in himself. Had he ever known this woman? Had his instincts about people he'd always felt confidence in been so off? He didn't know what kind of man she wanted, even now, but he'd pretty much come to the conclusion he was not and could never be it. Not if he wanted to be able to live with himself.

"We've got forty-odd calves to work before we quit today," he said, turning Gringo. "Let's get at it. You've got a job to do, Jamey," he added in a voice devoid of inflection.

He couldn't see her expression, shaded by the brim of her hat. The droop of her shoulders told the story of her own discouragement. Yet she nodded and said, "Yessir."

Chapter Ten

In the twilight shadows Kell leaned against the corral fence, separate from the party forming under the cottonwood. It was a perfect evening for a celebration, and Plum Creek had something to celebrate. The calf crop was a solid one, healthy and uniform. Few unbred cows had had to be culled and the fall crop looked good. The spring rains had been plentiful, guaranteeing a good summer in which to put some decent weight on the youngsters. God and fall cattle prices willing, Plum Creek would go on. Kell knew he'd conquered—for now, at least—the wild and woolly Panhandle. He'd done his best and it was a damned fine job, earning the respect of his men.

But somehow he'd failed to win the regard of the one person he most wanted.

He took a swig of beer and tried to drum up enthusiasm for the entertainment getting under way. People sat on bales of hay that had been pulled into a circle or on the tailgates of pickups. Who'd have thought Charley would have a fine baritone voice, which he put to good use singing one old favorite after another, with Purdy strumming along on an old guitar. One of the neighbor fellows provided a lonesome-sounding counterpoint on a harmonica. Josh and Kit clowned, looping an arm around the other's shoulder and putting their heads together as they tried to harmonize, ending up sounding more like coyotes howling at the moon. They'd brought out the town girls they were dating and it wasn't long before someone fetched the radio from the kitchen as people abandoned the oldies to dance to the hot, young country playing. The two girls were constantly breathless, as there was a dearth of female dance partners. Glenna and Jamey had yet to join the festivities. Kell had noticed their pickup was gone, and he wondered if they'd left for the evening. Perhaps to look for McSween?

The beer soured in his mouth. He wished to God he understood what was going on with Jamey Dunn. He'd thought over their conversations, especially the one just last night, when he'd kissed her and held her here under the stars. He'd known then as surely as he knew his own name that he and Jamey were of one accord. The respect—and yes, the love—between them had been so strong and sure.

So where had he been wrong? How had he failed?

As if conjured from his thoughts, Jamey appeared, walking with that loose, leggy gait of hers across the yard toward them, and all eyes seemed to stick on her. She wore a calf-length denim skirt that showed off her slim shape and emphasized her glorious height. Her red hair was loose, swirling around her shoulders in the light breeze. Tucked into the skirt was a Western-style shirt of the same sage green as her eyes and trimmed with beads. Part of the sensation, Kell knew, was because this look was so different from the usual jeans-and-boots Jamey Dunn. But most of it was because she was not just unusual, but beautiful.

Kell swallowed, but he didn't glance away.

She looked neither right nor left but came straight to stand in front of him. Her full lips parted tentatively, then pressed together, then parted again. "Kell, I... There's so much I want to tell you."

He merely raised his eyebrows, trying to remain aloof, to keep her from seeing the doubts that would forever assail him. Trying not to care, while still, one last time, trying to be the kind of cowboy she wanted.

Then she looked up at him with that combination of desperation and determination he'd seen in her from the first. "Dance with me?" she whispered, and hell if he didn't fall for her all over again.

He set down his beer bottle and wrapped an arm firmly around her waist. Her left hand rose to clutch his shoulder. Her right spread against his chest, and he hooked his fingers under hers, his thumb brushing against her knuckles.

They swayed, barely moving, in a shadowy pocket of privacy, and Kell would have killed to remain in that moment forever. But she had something to say.

"You said once, we are who we are," Jamey began softly, and he nodded. "Well, a year ago, I was searching for somethin', but I didn't know what. Now I know I was looking for myself and who I really was, who I wanted to be. My daddy always told me that I could be whatever I wanted to." She paused, as if in a bid for control or courage. "But he didn't want to let me go, to see if I could. And I worked it around in my mind to thinkin' he didn't believe in me, which made me not believe in myself."

Kell could feel the tension in her. This was hard for her, saying these things. Almost of its own volition, the hand spread on her back pressed firmly to her spine. *Go on*, it said.

She moved closer, her gaze fastened on his shoulder as they danced. "So I sort of threw the baby out with the bathwater, you know? I thought all I could be was a cowgirl. I'd never trained for anything else. I focused on that, and I kind of slighted the other things my daddy taught me, more than cowboying. Things like bein' fair and honest and honorable. Both my parents gave me a fine upbringing that way. Daddy sheltered me, though. It was purely natural for him to do that. But we parted at odds, and I never got the chance to work things out with him.''

Her voice had dropped to an agonized whisper, and Kell had to bend his head down to hear her, his jaw brushing her temple. "Go on," he said.

"It took me a while to start believing in myself again. That's because I made some pretty big mistakes. I married Henry McSween when I shouldn't have." She shook her head slightly, bumping his chin. "It was for all the wrong reasons on both sides. I knew real soon it wasn't going to work out, and I left to come home. But my daddy died, and then the ranch went, too, 'cause Momma and I couldn't keep it going. She broke her ankle tryin' to do it all, because I was—"

Jamey made a choking sound, her fingers tightening on his arm. "Oh, Kell, it just seemed like this one mistake got bigger and bigger as things kept happening. I knew it wasn't my fault Daddy died or we lost the ranch, but still—"

Kell pressed her cheek against his shoulder. Throughout her confession, his ire had slowly diminished, to be replaced by that tug on his emotions she always elicited in him. "I'm sorry, sweetheart. I knew you'd had it rough, and that you were hurting." He lifted her chin. Her mouth trembled and, though her eyes were dry, she looked on the verge of tears. She had yet to cry in front of him, but he knew as he knew his own heart that she'd shed many a tear. "You're a strong woman, Jamey. What's done is done, and you've put your life back together. Don't you think so?"

She nodded jerkily. "All except for one thing."

Kell's gut twisted. "McSween." He hesitated, wondering if he wanted to know, yet needing to. "Jamey, I just don't understand what you see in him."

"I don't see anything," she said, surprising him. "Once I thought because he was good at rodeoing that he was a good cowboy. And since the only cowboy I knew was my daddy, I credited him with my daddy's grit right off the bat.

But I hope I know more about people than I did a year ago. Whatever Henry McSween is, he's no cowboy."

His heart lifted even as he puzzled aloud, "Then why did you want him to stay today?"

"Because he doesn't know, Kell. And he needs to."

"Know what?" he asked, feeling a sense of *déjà vu.*

"Not what. Who." She took a deep breath and said on its rush out of her lungs, "Our baby. Hettie."

Kell stiffened in shock. He dropped the arms that held her and sank back against the fence post. "You've got a *baby?*"

Now Jamey stiffened. "I know I should have told you before, but see how you're reacting? I—I'm sorry. Maybe it wasn't fair. But I felt I had to keep Hettie a secret, even though I never meant to forever."

His head was spinning as bits and pieces of scenes came back to him, flashes of insight. "In the restaurant that Sunday," he said. "Was that…Hettie, with your mother?" Jamey nodded. "Then when I said I thought you'd make a good mother, you already were one."

She nodded again, her gaze growing soft. "And that was one of the nicest things anyone ever said to me."

He'd meant it. He thought of the feelings he'd experienced in his bedroom as she'd so naturally tended both his bruised body and ego. Another impression hit him. "Your clothes when you started here, the way you—" He gestured toward his shirtfront.

"I was nursin' Hettie," Jamey conceded.

Kell rubbed the back of his neck, trying to put the puzzle together. From the very first he'd sensed something about her at a basic level, to which he'd responded just as basically. And now, the image of Jamey with a child to her breast… Those almost overwhelming possessive, predatory and protective urges came upon him, all at once. Had there been some primitive instinct at play in the relationship between them? Had he known something subconsciously? He'd always put such stock in his intuitions about people, but this was a bit fantastic. He *couldn't* have known she was a mother.

But he had known she had qualities to be a mother. A good mother.

"Where's Hettie now?" he asked.

For some reason she bristled at that. "She's well taken care of. She's never lacked for attention."

"So you didn't tell me about her because you thought I'd slot you into a role? You're a mother, therefore you can't be something else?"

"Are you sayin' you wouldn't have?" She set her hands on her slim hips. "You'd already decided a woman couldn't cowboy. Even after you said that, I wanted to tell you. You had a right to know. But you were so blamed protective, just like my daddy. I could see you didn't believe in me!"

No, it dawned on Kell, he hadn't. Because he hadn't believed in himself then. And now? Was he fooling himself—still? Had he learned only to walk the walk and talk the talk of a cowboy, convinced himself that he was doing right by his land, his animals and the people who depended on him?

Did Jamey have faith in him?

"Do you still think I don't believe in you?" he asked urgently.

"No, you've been fair, given me a chance to prove myself."

"Then why didn't you still say anything?"

"Because you'd told me about your own daddy and momma neglectin' you." She laid her hand on his arm. "My heart broke for you, Kell—but it broke for my own little girl, too. I was already torn up with guilt about leaving her—even though Momma cared for her like Hettie was her own. But *I'm* Hettie's mother, and I was afraid you'd think badly of me if you knew I'd left my baby, put my own concerns first, over Hettie. I didn't, though," she said desperately.

Jamey let go of his arm to grasp the fence railing next to him in her hands. Though the light was dim, he could see her knuckles turn white. His own were clenched at his sides.

"I was tryin' to be the kind of person she could look up to, because I knew I was going to make mistakes raisin' her, no matter what I did to prevent them. And I wanted to be someone she could look past the faults and weaknesses, and love anyway. For... for *me*."

Kell stared at her. The words were the very ones carved on his own heart. He understood what she'd been struggling with, because her struggle was his. He could see where she'd gotten the idea he'd judge her harshly for leaving Hettie, for he'd judged his own parents. Even if he told himself he understood their neglect, it still affected him, or he wouldn't have made it his quest to step into Bud Hamilton's shoes.

But that aim had changed. It had taken Jamey to show him that there was more to being a cowboy than physical strength or endurance or even experience. Those qualities were certainly important, but a person could have their own unique skills and qualities and be a good cowboy, too. As he was. As Jamey was.

"Jamey," Kell said softly. "Can you believe I'm able to do the same? Love you... for you?"

At his question, her full lower lip quivered. Still, he saw, she didn't want to trust. "I don't know. I couldn't know." Her chin dropped. "I-I'd been wrong before, you see. About cowboys. That's why I've got to leave now, Kell."

"Leave?"

"Henry needs to know about his daughter. I've put off telling him long enough. And if there's a mistake that I own, that's the one."

She turned to face him. "I spent the past few hours packin'. Momma'll be back with Hettie in a few minutes. She'll take care of things for you while I'm gone. Hopefully, it won't be for long. I'm not made to be on the road day in, day out. But I will be back. I intend to do the job you've entrusted to me," she said with the formality she'd used in accepting the position on Plum Creek, and he sensed her withdrawing from him, which set off an alarm in him. She did this when threatened. "I know you'll be fair, even now that I've told you about Hettie, even if you can't... can't..."

"Can't love you?" he finished. "Jamey, I'm telling you—"

She pressed trembling fingers to his lips. "Don't say anything else. Not now. Wait until I've found Henry and settled what I have to with him. Then, if you still feel the same..."

That was the point! And that was why she couldn't leave! The trust, the connection between them seemed so very tenuous right now, he feared it would disintegrate completely.

She must have seen the argument in his eyes, for she begged, "Kell, please."

He pulled her hand away. "All right. I do promise you've got your job for as long as you want it. Don't worry about that. But tell me what you expect from McSween if you find him?"

"I—I don't know." Her eyes filled with the same fear he'd encountered in her that first day. "He wasn't much of a husband or cowboy, but maybe he'd be a good father. He has a right to try. I need to be fair, give him a chance."

Again, Kell grew alarmed. Was she going back to McSween—just because he was Hettie's father? Surely she saw that couldn't be best for either her or her baby. Kell didn't need a personality analysis to know that McSween was no good, and he would do Jamey no good. Had already, in fact. And now? What would happen when she told McSween of his daughter? Kell remembered the way the guy had touched her, his hand circling her ankle.

Once more, that basic urge reared its three ugly, harpy-like heads: predatory, protective, possessive. That need to conquer and control that Kell suddenly realized had far less to do with being a cowboy than being a man. Part of Kell tried to fight these impulses; part of him listened to the voice in his head that whispered of how McSween had charmed her once. Would he do it again? It'd be just like the jerk to pretend to have an interest in his daughter to get back in Jamey's good graces. Or to get back at Kell. And he didn't know if she'd be able to see through McSween in her desire to be fair to her daughter.

"I won't let you go, Jamey," Kell vowed suddenly, not caring if he sounded like her father or even chauvinist of the century.

She looked at him as if she could see clear through to the heart of him, and understood him completely. "Kell," she said sadly. "You can't stop me."

"Then you tell me what I'm supposed do!" he blazed.

Her answer took the starch right out of him. "You can go on believin' in me, that I've always tried to do my best. You're an honorable, decent man, Kell Hamilton. I don't know if I still have your regard after what I've told you, but I'm not going to stop trying to live up to it." Now she really looked ready to cry. "Goodbye, Kell."

She started to walk away. *Make her stay!* his every instinct screamed at him. He could do it, and not through physical force. He could convince her, overcome her reservations with coaxing words and cowboy phrases. But he guessed that had been McSween's technique.

It was on the tip of his tongue to tell her he loved her, to ask her to marry him and let him be a proper father to Hettie. Maybe then she wouldn't go.

Instead, Kell's hand shot out and, without thinking, he grasped Jamey's arm, brought her around and flush against him, producing a gasp from her. He took that advantage, sealing her lips with his mouth. Her taste was warm and irresistible, and he pressed for more. She stiffened briefly before grasping him behind the neck to bring him closer still.

And with every bone in his body, Kell knew he could make her stay. She made a choking sound in the back of her throat, and he pulled back just enough to see into Jamey's sage-colored eyes, brilliant with unshed tears. She knew it, too. He could make her stay without one word, not by possessing her or conquering her, but through the physical and

spiritual link which had always existed between them, from
the very first. Their hearts had known each other even then,
for they both yearned for the same thing.

And that was why Kell found himself saying hoarsely,
"Remember this, that's all I ask. When you find McSween,
show him the daughter you bore him, do what you have to.
But don't forget this understanding we've always had between us."

Abruptly, he released her. "Now go."

It was the hardest thing Kell had ever done, watching
Jamey walk away.

Then she stopped dead in her tracks, and he saw what
they'd been too involved to notice before: Henry McSween
had returned to Plum Creek.

Jamey stared at the familiar figure swaggering into the
circle of people. Everyone, including the dancers, had come
to a standstill, as if frozen in time. Henry had nerve, she'd
give him that. His showing up would certainly save her time
and trouble, but she had a notion it wouldn't balance out the
additional grief it would cause.

Out of the corner of her eye, she saw Kell step forward,
righteousness in every line of his body. This was his ranch
and he'd told Henry never to step foot on it again. He had
a right to protect his interests. Right then, Kell reminded her
of her father. No, he wouldn't have prevented her from going after Henry, but it was too much to expect any man to
stand by and watch her greet the father of her child. Would
she blame him if he threw her ex-husband off his land?
Wouldn't it be easier for all of them if she let him?

"Kell, please," she said in a low voice.

He stared at her, and she saw that he was more than just
righteous. He was afraid—for her. And in a flash she realized the threat Henry's return posed: Henry obviously
wanted something bad enough to risk Kell's wrath. It had to
be her.

Jamey experienced a little of her own righteous anger. She had a will of her own.

She stayed Kell with one look, two words. *"Trust me."*

His jaw clenched and unclenched, and for a moment she thought he'd ignore her request. Then he nodded. She knew what that cost him, and she loved him more than ever.

Henry spotted her and sauntered over. His hat was tipped back on his head, making him look younger than his twenty-three years. She wondered what she'd ever seen in a boy like him.

"What do you want, Henry?" she asked.

He smiled his charming smile, gold tooth and all, and spread his hands in front of him. "Why, darlin', I'm here to give you what *you* want. Seemed like today you might've fancied havin' me hang around." He raised his eyebrows inculpably at Kell, who stood a few paces behind and off to one side of Jamey.

"Truth to tell, I am glad you're here," she said.

"I knew it!" he crowed, throwing a full-fledged smirk at Kell, who might be letting her handle this, but that didn't stop him from shooting daggers at Henry with his eyes.

Which made Henry fidget, just for a moment. "Y'know, I could use a little exercise." He cocked an arm at Jamey. "Care to show these yokels how to really scoot a boot?"

"You mean, dance?" She shook her head. "No thanks, Henry."

His smile faded a little, but not much. "Ah, come on, darlin'. 'Member how we danced together?"

"Oh, I remember. You were a fine one for sweepin' a girl 'round the floor with your fancy steps. One of the best. But dancing isn't everything, Henry."

He must have seen something subduing in her expression—or Kell's—for he dropped his arm to his side. "Well, surely you remember how we *really* danced?" he asked, low and suggestive.

Jamey took a step forward, putting herself more squarely between her ex-husband and Kell. "Don't be crude, Henry," she said firmly.

But, unbelievably, he went on. "Remember how we got engaged and married and bedded all in one night. Weren't we something together?"

"No, *we* weren't. We were never partners, in the true sense. I'm not going to say it was all your fault, but you never had any intention of staying married to me, and that wasn't right." Her anger became indignant. "Why'd you even do it if you didn't mean for it to last?"

"Jamey, darlin'." He shifted on his feet, a side-step that mirrored his words. "I didn't see how I could resist you, pure and simple. You were so pretty and fresh—"

"I'm tired of the sweet talkin', Henry! I think I know why you married me, even if you've never bothered to search your conscience to figure it out. I was a challenge, just like some bronc that needs busting or calf that needs roping. You never loved me, and when it comes right down to it, I never loved you." Here was the last of her regrets, the last of her apologies. "I used you, too, to rush headlong into life. To run...from myself. It was wrong, and I'd like to apologize for that."

"You would? I mean—" Henry puffed up his chest. "I forgive you, darlin'. It's all water under the bridge."

"I wish it were, Henry," Jamey said sorrowfully. "I truly wish it were."

Behind her came the crunch of gravel under tires. Jamey turned to see her pickup pull into the drive. It came to a stop and her mother got out of the driver's side and went around to open the passenger door. Jamey, Kell, Henry, and most everyone else, watched as Glenna hefted something into her arms. She straightened, and there, a chubby fist in her mouth and looking adorable in a romper made from the same material as Jamey's shirt, was Hettie.

Her hair had grown out about an inch, and it curled around her head in a coppery halo backlit by the porch light.

As Glenna approached, Jamey could see the baby wore an expression of apprehension at the unfamiliar sights and sounds. Before, the crowd had at least pretended not to listen to the confrontation taking place; now, though, people frankly stared.

Jamey stepped forward, arms extended. "There's my girl," she said, and felt a rush of happiness as Hettie focused on her and her voice. The baby's face cleared. She kicked impatiently and held her own small arms out to her mother.

Sweeping her daughter into her embrace with a big kiss, she whispered, "Oh, sugar, I've missed you." Jamey met her own mother's warm, loving gaze, read the encouragement there. Then she closed her eyes briefly, praying for strength to get through these next few moments. *Let me know what's right. Let me do what's right.*

She turned and caught Kell's gaze on her. The look in his eyes, so like the one he gave her that Sunday when he'd told her she'd make a good mother, went straight to her feminine core. He was seeing her for the first time in this role, and she could tell it affected him in the most basic of ways.

And she knew why it did at this particular time. They were both going on instinct, and it was obvious he was this close to challenging Henry. Kell was a cowboy, after all. She almost wanted him to throw Henry off the ranch, sparing her this confrontation.

Somehow Jamey found the strength to walk forward with Hettie.

She stopped in front of Henry, his face a study of bafflement and disbelief. And trepidation.

"Henry, I'd like you to meet your daughter." She smoothed down the copper curls. "Henrietta McSween."

He stared at Hettie. She stared back, her forehead pocked with puckers. "My...daughter?"

"I know it's a shock." How different his reaction was from Kell's, who was at this moment watching Henry guardedly, protective of Jamey and Hettie. It seemed to her the two men were hardly of the same species, let alone gender. And she felt suddenly embarrassed to the roots of her soul for Kell to witness just how unsuitable this man was, whom she'd once chosen to be her mate and father of her children.

It was the last thing she wanted to do, but Jamey stalwartly asked, "Would you like to hold her?"

Henry actually backed up a step. His Adam's apple bobbed in a huge, uneasy swallow. "Is this why you wanted me to stay?"

"Yes. I felt you had a right to know your daughter. And she has a right to know her daddy. She's...she's as much yours as mine." Jamey hitched the baby higher on her hip. Hettie clung to the front of her mother's shirt, her apprehensive gaze still on Henry.

"So what *do* you want, Jamey?" Henry asked suspiciously, still making not one move toward his own child.

What did she want? God, she wanted to run, take Hettie as far away from this man as possible, and keep her safe forever. But that was impossible. Jamey couldn't keep her daughter safe forever. She'd learned that the hard way. Yet she knew then and there that she'd never consign care of her child over to him, even for an hour. He could visit, but that was all. "I thought you might like to put your hand in on raising her, is all."

At that, Henry's expression cleared. "Oh. Well, Jamey, I surely would enjoy that. But, shoot, I'm on the road all the time, darlin', so I guess you'll have to do most of the raisin' yourself. I hate to do that to you," he added, sounding not one bit sincere. "I'll send money when I can, even though you know I don't make a whole lot."

Jamey's gaze swept over his spanking new jeans and shirt, saw his restless look that said he wanted to be shed of this responsibility, too. His own child.

She'd thought she was through with regrets, but here came another, the strongest of all, for she saw truly the kind of man Henry McSween was and always would be. He had no intention, no instinct, to father. And she knew why she'd been so afraid to tell him about Hettie: her knowledge about people had told her that he'd be no more responsible toward his daughter than he was to his wife, while an even stronger instinct rejected the notion that a man could forsake his own child. On top of that was the lesson learned of being wrong about Henry before, and she hadn't trusted herself to be right about him now.

Apparently making her own decision about Henry, Hettie whimpered, turning away from her father and burying her face in the crook of her mother's neck. Jamey bent her head, her cheek pressed to Hettie's crown, to hide her sudden tears. Tears of relief, mainly, but also of that incredible regret. To have created a child with this man, something so wondrous and special, and have him dismiss them both so easily. . . .

She watched him continue backing away, as if she would come after him if he didn't keep an eye on her. She wanted to call him back, try to explain what he would miss. All the joy.

Out of the corner of her eye, Jamey spotted Glenna, and knew without actually seeing them, that there were tears in her mother's eyes, too. Tears of pride.

Yes, all the joy—and all the pain.

So she remained silent, rocking her baby. Because she and Hettie deserved better than the likes of Henry McSween. Fathering or birthing a child wasn't what made one a parent. It was being there for your child, loving them and supporting them, not just materially but with your faith and belief in them, knowing they'd have to live their own lives and make their own mistakes. And if there was any man that fit that description, it was Kell Hamilton. Had she destroyed his regard for her or any chance they had together with her doubts and lack of judgment?

Jamey turned to find him standing close behind her. She looked up in surprise as he grasped her upper arms.

"To hell with McSween," he said in a low, fierce voice. "He's not worth crying over. We can raise Hettie up right. On a ranch just like you were."

She stared in disbelief. "W-we?"

"I can take care of her. Neither of you would lack for anything. I may not be a real father, but neither was my uncle, and he was the best parent a kid could have. And I may not be the kind of rancher he was, but I'll make it work come hell or high water. I promise the same to you and Hettie."

She believed him. He *could* take care of them, but did he mean as her employer, or as...

"You're going to marry me and stay right here, Jamey Dunn," he ordered, cowboylike.

Jamey sniffed, then she smiled—no, grinned like a fool. "Yessir," she said dutifully, and Kell gave his own grin filled with relief.

Over his shoulder she noticed Henry slinking off. Kell turned and saw him, too. Kell threw a purely devilish look at Jamey before calling out, "What's that?" cocking his head as if to listen. "Sounds to me like the rumbling of half a ton of Hell Cow with blood in her eye."

Henry's shoulders hunched, and he whirled, wild-eyed.

"My mistake, McSween," Kell announced. "It was just your colossal ego lumbering after you."

The cowboys hooted. The music started up again, and people drifted away, giving Kell and Jamey—and Hettie— their privacy. Bent eye level with the baby, he said softly, "Hello there."

Her little mouth pursed, long-lashed eyes speculative. Then Hettie blinked and queried irresistibly, "Da?"

"Good God, am I going to have a situation on my hands in sixteen years." Kell hoisted her with his big hands, settling her in the crook of his arm. "Is this how to hold her?"

"You're doin' fine," Jamey said encouragingly as she arranged the ruffles on Hettie's front.

"Jamey, like I said, I know about as much about being a father as I did about ranching when I started, which I have a feeling I've still got a lot to learn. But you can always count on me to do my best."

"That's all I expect. And besides, there's two of us now. What you don't know, I do, and the other way around. That's the way it's supposed to be." She touched him, just a hand upon his arm, partly in the comfort and understanding she'd offered him before and would in the future. And partly for her own assurance that the connection that had always existed between them remained. It was as strong as ever. "We'll do fine, together."

Kell, chin tucked, and Hettie, wet fingers fastened to that chin, gazed at each other in mutual fascination. "McSween's an idiot to give this up," he muttered. His gaze switched to Jamey, scanning over her and making her tingle all over. "An idiot to give you up.

"Now," he said sternly, looping his free arm around her and bringing her against his side, "I'm going to tell you something I've been meaning to for weeks."

"What's that?"

"I love you, Jamey Dunn."

"Oh, Kell. I love you, too." Her husky voice cracked. "I so wanted Hettie to be able to tell people her daddy was a cowboy." She smiled at him. "Now, she will."

She saw how her words affected him, much as his always affected her, by giving him the confirmation he'd fought so hard for.

Then he said, "Only after she brags that her momma was a cowboy, too."

His brown eyes burned into hers as they swayed, though there was no song playing. Yet this was their dance. They felt its beat in their very souls. They listened to its message with their hearts. And they knew it would go on forever.

* * * * *

Silhouette
ROMANCE™

COMING NEXT MONTH

#1084 MAKE ROOM FOR BABY—Kristin Morgan
Bundles of Joy
Once, Camille Boudreaux and Bram Delcambre dreamed of marriage—until betrayal tore them apart. But with a new baby about to join them together as a family, would their love get a second chance?

#1085 DADDY LESSONS—Stella Bagwell
Fabulous Fathers
Joe McCann was about to fire Savanna Starr until he saw her skill at child rearing. Would helping this single dad raise his teenage daughter lead to a new job—as his wife?

#1086 WILDCAT WEDDING—Patricia Thayer
Wranglers and Lace
Nothing would get between Jessie Burke and her ranch. Not even dynamic oilman Brett Murdock. But Brett had more on his mind than Jessie's land. He wanted Jessie—for life.

#1087 HIS ACCIDENTAL ANGEL—Sandra Paul
Spellbound
Bree Smith was supposed to teach cynical Devlin Hunt about love—not fall for the handsome bachelor! What chance did an angel like her have with a man who didn't believe in miracles?

#1088 BELATED BRIDE—Charlotte Moore
Karen Haig had left her hometown a jilted bride years ago. Now she was back—and her former fiancé Seth Bjornson had a plan to make her stay. But could she trust her heart to Seth again?

#1089 A CONVENIENT ARRANGEMENT—Judith Janeway
Debut Author
Jo Barnett might be sharing a home with Alex MacHail but she wasn't going to share her life with him. Then Alex introduced her to his adorable little boy, and Jo found herself falling for father and son.

Take 4 bestselling love stories FREE

Plus get a FREE surprise gift!

Special Limited-time Offer

Mail to Silhouette Reader Service™

3010 Walden Avenue
P.O. Box 1867
Buffalo, N.Y. 14269-1867

YES! Please send me 4 free Silhouette Romance™ novels and my free surprise gift. Then send me 6 brand-new novels every month, which I will receive months before they appear in bookstores. Bill me at the low price of $2.19 each plus 25¢ delivery and applicable sales tax, if any.* That's the complete price and a savings of over 10% off the cover prices—quite a bargain! I understand that accepting the books and gift places me under no obligation ever to buy any books. I can always return a shipment and cancel at any time. Even if I never buy another book from Silhouette, the 4 free books and the surprise gift are mine to keep forever.

215 BPA ANRP

Name	(PLEASE PRINT)	
Address	Apt. No.	
City	State	Zip

This offer is limited to one order per household and not valid to present Silhouette Romance™ subscribers. *Terms and prices are subject to change without notice. Sales tax applicable in N.Y.

USROM-295   ©1990 Harlequin Enterprises Limited

Silhouette celebrates motherhood in May with...

Debbie Macomber
Jill Marie Landis
Gina Ferris Wilkins

in

Three Mothers & a Cradle

Join three award-winning authors in this beautiful collection you'll treasure forever. The same antique, hand-crafted cradle connects these three heartwarming romances, which celebrate the joys and excitement of motherhood. Makes the perfect gift for yourself or a loved one!

A special celebration of love,

Only from

Silhouette®

—where passion lives.

MD95

SOMETIMES, BIG SURPRISES COME IN SMALL PACKAGES!

Bundles of Joy

MAKE ROOM FOR BABY
by
Kristin Morgan

A beautiful widow, Camille Boudreaux was content to spend the rest of her life alone. But her peaceful existence was shaken when her only daughter, Skyler, fell in love and married Josh Delacambre, the only son of her first love, Bram. And soon Camille found that not only the pain of their thwarted love still lived, but the passion, as well....

Available in June, only from

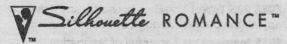

Silhouette ROMANCE™

BOJ2

Announcing
the New Pages & Privileges™ Program
from Harlequin® and Silhouette®

Get All This FREE
With Just One Proof-of-Purchase!

- **FREE Travel Service** with the guaranteed lowest available airfares plus 5% cash back on every ticket

- **FREE Hotel Discounts** of up to 60% off at leading hotels in the U.S., Canada and Europe

- **FREE Petite Parfumerie** collection (a $50 Retail value)

- **FREE $25 Travel Voucher** to use on any ticket on any airline booked through our Travel Service

- **FREE Insider Tips Letter** full of fascinating information and hot sneak previews of upcoming books

- **FREE Mystery Gift** (if you enroll before May 31/95)

And there are more great gifts and benefits to come!
Enroll today and become Privileged!

(see insert for details)

PROOF-OF-PURCHASE

Offer expires October 31, 1996

SR-PP1